RESCUING THE RANCHER

COWBOYS AND ANGELS

GEORGE MCVEY

CHAPTER 1

Marta Campbell sank onto the bench outside the train depot. The letter she had just read had officially ended her hope for the future.

Miss Campbell,

We were appalled to hear what had befallen you on your journey to us. We sympathize with you and rejoice that you escaped your captors without major harm. However, when you weren't at the train station when we came to meet you, we had no choice but to seek an immediate replacement for the position. There is no need for you to continue your journey to San Francisco as our need for a nanny has been met.

We wish you the best in your future endeavors.

Sincerely,

John and Caroline Forsythe.

She had no clue what to do next. She couldn't continue to stay with the Jacobs family. They were a sweet older couple, but she knew her staying with them was putting a stress on their resources. She'd prayed that the Forsythes would still need her, but now she knew that they didn't. Marta closed her eyes against the despair the words of the letter brought her. "What now, God?" she prayed.

"Well, if it were me, I'd go to the mercantile and get some lemon drops." The voice startled Marta, and she opened her eyes to see the old woman sitting beside her on the bench. "Excuse me?"

The older woman was dressed in a light gray travel dress, her face, while old and wrinkled, held a joy and peace unlike anything Marta had ever seen before. "You asked what now; I said if it were me I'd go get some lemon drops. They are your favorite, aren't they, Marta?"

Marta's mouth dropped open. "How do you know who I am? Or that my favorite candy is lemon drops?"

The woman smiled at her. "I know everything there is to know about you, Marta Campbell. I'm your angel."

Marta's eyes got large; this woman had to be a bit senile. "I am not crazy and you are not imagining me. I'm an angel, and I've been assigned to you for the foreseeable future."

Marta slid as far to the end of the bench as she could. "Umm... all right... So you're my angel and your answer to me asking God what to do now that my life is a mess is to go buy some lemon drops?"

The woman smiled. "I can see you don't believe me, but the answer is yes, that's what you should do next. Just because the path you thought you were set on has ended doesn't mean there isn't another path you should be following." The woman rose and took a step to stand in front of Marta. Marta started as the stationmaster walked right through the woman like she wasn't even there. Marta shook her head. Maybe she was sleeping, and this was all a nightmare.

The woman placed her hands on her hips and sighed. "Pinch yourself."

"What?"

"I want you to pinch yourself so you know you are not dreaming. Now hurry; you are running out of time."

Marta frowned. "Running out of time for what?"

"To find the path you should be on. Oh for heaven's sake, here." The woman reached down and pinched Marta on the back of her hand.

"Ouch!"

"Now you know you aren't asleep or dreaming, and no you aren't going crazy. Now get yourself down to the mercantile and buy that candy. Keep your eyes open on the way, too. When God closes one door, he always opens another. So look for it." The woman started to walk away when she suddenly turned back, "Oh, and no matter how crazy it may sound you should accept any proposal that might come your way today."

Marta jumped to her feet. "What?"

But the woman had disappeared as if she'd never been there.

Marta didn't know what to think except maybe the woman had been her angel. It would be just like her to get an angel who spoke in riddles and gave useless advice. However, she had nothing else to do and, oddly enough, some lemon drops did sound like a good way to soothe her disappointment while she tried to figure out what to do next. Maybe she'd see if there were any recent newspapers from Denver at the mercantile. While she was there, she needed to start looking for another option besides living off the charity of the townspeople of Creede or Bachelor, kind as they had been.

As she neared the mercantile, she saw a wagon

with several children out front. There was no adult to be seen, and the children, well two of the children, seemed to be roughhousing in the back. Two boys, by the looks of things, and they had the wagon rocking with their antics. Shouldn't someone have been watching them? The oldest was a girl and she didn't look old enough to be trying to watch out for the others. Where were their parents?

Just then, the bigger boy shoved and the younger one flipped over the back of the wagon and landed on the hard-packed road behind the wagon. Marta ran up and took the small child in her arms. "My goodness, are you okay?"

The child in her arms started crying, and the older boy in the wagon called out, "I'm sorry, Randy. I'm sorry! I didn't mean to throw you outta the wagon." Then he was crying, too. The older girl climbed down to stand beside Marta, who still was holding the little boy in her arms. "Are you hurt, honey?"

The girl gave her a look that would curdle milk. "His name is Randy and he's fine. He's had worse spills than that."

"Where are your parents? They shouldn't have left you all out here alone. What if your brother had fallen to the right and under a passing wagon or horse?"

The little girl put her hands on her hips. "I was watching them."

"Yes, but you shouldn't be alone like this; anything could happen."

Before the girl could say anything more, the door to the mercantile opened and a man with red hair and a beard hurried over. He placed a large box in the back of the wagon before rounding to where Marta was still kneeling, holding the young boy and wiping his tears. "What's going on here, Rachel?"

Marta stood with the boy still in her arms. "Are these your children?"

"Yes."

"What is the meaning of leaving them out here unsupervised? Your son fell out of the wagon and got hurt. Thankfully, he fell out of the back and not over the side where he could have been struck by a passing wagon. What kind of father are you, anyway?"

"An overwhelmed one, Miss...?"

"Campbell, Marta Campbell." That was when she noticed that the man's face was haggard like he hadn't had much sleep. In the arm that hadn't been balancing the box of goods from the store was a very small baby, no older than a few months. "Where is your wife, Mister?"

All the children started crying at her question. What in the world?

The man's eyes went hard. "Clark. And for your information, Miss Campbell, my wife passed away two months ago. We are doing the best we can under the circumstances."

Marta gasped at his declaration. "I'm sorry for your loss, Mr. Clark. I didn't know, but you still can't be leaving your children to themselves like this. Your son could have been seriously hurt."

Mr. Clark's face, what she could see of it under his scruffy beard, turned as red as his hair. "Look here, we're doing the best we can. If for one minute you think you could take care of my family better than I've been, then marry me and prove it."

Marta's mouth dropped open in shock. She caught a movement on the boardwalk behind Mr. Clark and looked to see the old woman, her angel, nodding and mouthing, *"Yes! Say yes!"*

She looked back at the man and the five children watching them. "All right, I will. Take us to the Reverend's house."

Now it was the man's mouth that dropped open. "What??"

Marta lifted the boy she held into the back of the wagon and then pointed to the man. "You said if I thought I could take better care of your family than you have been, to marry you and prove it. So I shall! Take us to Reverend Bing, and let's get married." She turned and looked at the little red-haired girl still standing beside her. "Can you get in the wagon on your own, Rachel, or do you need help?"

The girl glared at her. "I don't need nothing from you."

"Then get in the wagon; we have places to go."

The girl looked up at her father. "Pa?"

The man nodded then turned his attention to Marta again. "Are you serious? You want to get married today? Right now?"

She looked him in the eye and held her arms out to take the infant. He placed it automatically in her arms. "Yes, I'm serious. It is obvious you need the help and, honestly, I was just wondering what I was going to do with myself. I think God put us in the same place to help us both. So let's go see the Reverend and get this over with."

She climbed up into the seat on the wagon and settled the baby in her arms. After a few minutes, Mister Clark came around and climbed up into the seat beside her. He looked at her again like he couldn't believe she was sitting there beside him before he took up the reins. With one last look at his four children in the back, "You young'uns sit still now. We're going to Bachelor before we go home."

"Why, Pa?" The oldest girl asked. "We don't need her help."

"Yes, we do, Rachel. You're doing the best you can, but you're still a little girl yourself."

"I don't want her to help us."

"That's enough, Rachel. I said she's coming to help us and take care of you and your brothers and sisters, and that's the way it is."

"Fine, but I'm not gonna call her Ma. 'Cause she ain't our ma!"

Marta looked at the girl. "That's fine, Rachel. How about you just call me Marta. I know I'm not your ma, and I won't try to take her place, but let me help take care of your Pa and family. Will that be okay?"

The girl scowled and crossed her arms. "I reckon since Pa says so."

"Thank you." Marta gave the girl a smile and then looked at the man she was going to be marrying as he got the wagon started and turned to head up to Bachelor. "Since I'm going to be marrying you, don't you think I should know your first name?"

The man sighed. "Reckon so. It's Royce. Royce Clark."

"It's nice to meet you, Royce. I'm Marta."

Royce nodded and then turned his attention to the road ahead of them.

"Just so you know, I'm not sure I can offer you a normal loving marriage. I mean, my Lucy isn't but two months gone."

Marta looked down at the little child in her arms. "I understand that. I'm not asking you for your heart, Royce. Honestly, I'm one of the women who was abducted. I'm sure you knew that. I lost a live-in position as a nanny by being taken. While the people here have been kind, I can't keep living off of their charity. I figure what you are offering me isn't much different than what I would have been doing as a nanny. Only it gives me a house to run as well. As for love, I gave up on that a while ago."

"Well, I just wanted you to know. I'll do the best I can for you, and you'll always have a home, but my heart still belongs to Lucy. It always will."

"I understand. Please don't worry about that."

"All right then. I guess I should tell you we have a ranch on the other side of Creede about an hour out. I have several cowboys and other ranch hands who work for me. I'll introduce you, but for the most part, they'll not be a bother to you."

"All right. Umm, it might be a good idea if I knew the children's names and ages."

"I reckon it might," Royce said with a small smile. Marta's heart did a little flip in her chest. Even with just that small smile, it was obvious her soon-to-be husband was handsome. At twenty-seven, she'd given up on ever finding a husband, even a plain looking one. So to be sitting beside this man who could make her heart beat like this was strange. She'd have to be extra careful not to let her heart lead her into love. She had no desire to love a man who had just admitted he'd never be able to return that love. She would be content with caring for him and his children.

"The oldest is Rachel, as you already know. She is nine. She's had to step up after her mother passed. Then next is Royce Junior, we call him RJ. He's seven, and he's a handful. I don't know where it comes from, but that boy is all energy from the moment he gets up until the moment he falls asleep. Lucy used to say he was a tornado wrapped in a boy-sized package. Then there's Randy. He's four; he's the one you were holding when I came out of the store. He's not as bad as RJ, but he does any and everything RJ tells him to do. Plus, he will question you about everything. He wants to know why everything happens and how it all works. As much as RJ's body runs nonstop, Randy's mouth does the same thing. Then there's Rose, she's not yet two. She's very independent, wants to do it all herself. And you're holding Raeann, Lucy died giving birth to her. I almost lost her, too, but Doc had some newfangled formula for helping feed babies. There's some in a bag in the back and more at the house. Let me know when we get down to one crate of it so I can order more. It has to come from somewhere back east."

Marta nodded. "I will, I'm familiar with that formula solution. My last employer was a doctor and mentioned how it would be lifesaving in cases like yours."

"Tell me about yourself. I mean, if we're going to try to live together as husband and wife, I should know a little something about you."

Marta shrugged. "There isn't much to tell. I grew up in an orphanage. I don't know who my parents are. I was found on the stoop of a church with a note that had my name and age on it, not much else. When I turned eighteen, the headmistress of the orphanage told me she procured me a position with a local family as their nanny. I stayed until their boys turned old enough not to need me anymore. Then I had just secured a job as a nanny in San Francisco, which sounded like an adventure to me. That's what brought me west. I got off the train at the stop here in Creede to stretch my legs and get some foodstuff for the rest of the trip, when someone grabbed me and put a cloth over my mouth. When I woke up, I was in a root cellar with three other women. We were held there for several weeks, and more women were thrown in the cellar from time to time. As I'm sure you heard, we escaped the day of the big fire that took out half the town. I sent a telegram to my employer to let them know what had happened and got a letter from them today telling me that, while they are sorry for what befell me, they had filled the position when I didn't show up. That's when I ran into your children and you."

Royce looked at her with admiration in his eyes. "You've had quite a life, Marta Campbell. How old are you anyway?

She looked at the man beside her. "A gentleman should never ask a lady her age, sir, but since we are to be married I will tell you. I'm twenty-seven."

They had arrived in Bachelor as they talked and were pulling to a stop in front of the church. "Well, I'm thirty-one so that's good; we're not that far apart. I'll go see if Reverend Bing can do a wedding today."

"I'll need to go by the Jacobs as well and get my things. If he can, that is."

Royce nodded and looked at the kids in the back. "You all stay with Miss Campbell and mind your manners."

A chorus of "Yes, Pa" had Marta smiling at her new family. She took a deep breath as she watched Royce walk up to the parsonage and knock. She saw Reverend Bing and Royce talk, and then the Reverend gave a nod and went inside. Royce walked back to them. "Let's go get your things. Reverend Bing said school will be out in about half an hour, and he'll get his sister and Mrs. Fontaine to stand as witnesses. He figured that maybe some of the mothers would stay as well. It seems you've made some friends here."

Marta nodded. "I would like to think so."

They headed up the loop to the Jacobs' little cottage. It wouldn't take long for Marta to pack her things and say goodbye to the older couple. She figured they'd insist on coming down to the church as well. Sure enough, as soon as they heard what was happening, they started making their way down to the church. All that was left was to walk down that aisle and say I do. With one final look at the place she'd stayed the last few weeks and the closest thing to a home she'd ever had, Marta shut the door and allowed Royce to help her up into the wagon. With just two simple words, for the first time in her life, Marta would have a family and a home. All because she listened to an angel.

CHAPTER 2

Royce looked at the woman standing beside him. He'd started the day mourning his beloved Lucy and trying to take care of his children, and now he was about to marry a complete stranger who thought she could take better care of his family than he could. Trouble was, she probably could. He'd managed to keep them fed for the last two months since Lucy had passed, but they were getting tired of beans and bacon sandwiches. It was the only two things he knew how to cook, and he could only do the sandwiches if he had gone to the mercantile and bought bread.

Marta had told him she grew up in an orphanage. He knew that most orphanages taught the young girls to do domestic chores. It was one way they helped keep the cost of caring for the kids low. So she could probably cook and clean. She'd also worked as a nanny for a society family back east which meant she'd know how to care for the children. He'd thank God tonight for the good luck that had come his way today. A simple phrase spoken in anger had been an answer to the prayer he wouldn't even allow himself to pray, someone to make his life a little easier by caring for his house and children. He'd have hired someone but there weren't any older women in Creede that he'd trust with his kids all day. That God had dropped Marta in his path seemed like a wonderful thing

She wasn't bad looking, either. A little larger than his Lucy had been and her curves were more pronounced. Nevertheless, Marta wasn't unpleasant to look at. She just wasn't Lucy. Therein lay his only concern. He was about to vow to love, honor, and cherish this woman. While he was sure he would honor and cherish her, he wasn't sure his heart could ever come to love her. She just wasn't Lucy.

Reverend Bing cleared his throat and Royce realized he was supposed to be responding. "Oh! Umm... I do."

"Then I now pronounce you man and wife. You can kiss your bride."

Everyone laughed when Randy cried out, "Eww, don't do it, Pa!"

Marta blushed, and he realized that she was very pretty. Not a classic beauty like Lucy but very pleasant to look at. The blush caused the smattering of freckles across her checks to stand out. He quickly lowered his head to hers and brushed her lips in a chaste but sweet kiss. He pulled back a bit quickly and saw that his children were all watching them closely. Rachel had her arms crossed and was scowling so hard he thought she'd combust from the anger obvious on her face. RJ just looked confused, and Randy was making a face like he'd been asked to eat some kind of green vegetable. Rose and Raeann were the only ones not affected by the impromptu wedding they'd just had. Both were too young to know what was going on.

The people who had stayed to witness their vows were gathering around Marta and him and congratulating them. He smiled and accepted the handshakes of the men, and Marta was drawn away by the women and hugged. She didn't let them pull her too far away and the first thing she did was take both Rose and Raeann in her arms, Rose on her left hip and Raeann in the crook of her right arm held against her body. She looked like she'd been taking care of them all her life. She saw him heading toward the entrance of the church, and she called out to the children. "Rachel, will you please get your brothers and the three of you go get in the wagon; your Pa is ready to go."

Rachel looked at Marta and snarled, "Don't tell me what to do. You aren't my ma. I don't have to listen to you."

Royce turned and looked at his daughter, shocked that she would use that tone with any adult. "Rachel Clark, you know better than to speak to a grownup like that! You will listen to Marta. She may not be your ma, but she is the woman who will be taking care of you from this day forward. You will obey her just like you did your ma or you and I will go have a discussion behind the woodpile. Do you understand me, young lady?"

She clenched her jaw, and her blue eyes sparked with anger. "Yes, sir."

"Good, now do as you were told."

She grabbed RJ and Randy by the hands and jerked them toward the door. "Come on; we have to do what that lady says. Let's get in the wagon."

Royce started to say something when Marta quietly called his name. He turned, and she shook her head. "Let her be. She is upset. She obeyed, so leave her be. Let me handle her attitude my way. She just needs some time and space to get used to me."

"She's being disrespectful; that isn't right."

Marta smiled at him. "I know, but for now let me deal with her disrespect my way. If she disobeys me, I will allow you to handle it. Otherwise, please allow me to take care of it."

He stared at the woman he'd just married, and even though he didn't know her well yet, he could see the concern and determination in her face. Concern for his daughter and determination that she would handle the situation her own way. He nodded. "Fine, you deal with Rachel your way. However, I will expect you to inform me if she refuses to obey you. I won't tolerate that. I won't allow the disrespect for long, either, so get it fixed quickly."

Marta nodded and smiled at him. "Thank you. We should get to the wagon, too. I expect we still have a way to go to reach your ranch. I'd like to be there before dark and see what all I need to start doing tomorrow."

Royce held out his hands and took Rose from her and settled her on his hip just like Marta had been carrying her. Then he held out his arm for Marta to take and escorted her to the wagon. He sat Rose up

in the back with her sister and brothers and helped
Marta up onto the bench seat. He went around and
climbed up, and saw that Marta lifted Rose up to sit
between them on the bench. The toddler had
scooted up against his new wife who had placed her
arm around the little girl. Raeann was nestled snug
in her arms and Royce's heart skipped a little at how
much like his new wife his two younger children
looked. He figured that both girls would only know
Marta as their mother. Rose was too young and the
memory of Lucy would fade from her mind. Raeann
would only ever know Marta as her mother. That
thought saddened him but, at the same time, it gave
him a feeling of peace that they would at least know
a mother's care. Even if she wasn't the woman who
gave them birth.

They rode to the ranch with Marta talking
mostly over her shoulder to the children sitting
behind them. Royce listened as she asked them about
chores they had, what they liked to eat, and other
things that she would want to know as the person
looking after them. Rachel answered her, but grudg-
ingly. RJ and Randy seemed happy she was talking to
them. Royce sat listening as he drove them home. He
was impressed with how Marta treated each of his
three older children. She asked questions and

allowed them to ask her questions. She answered each one. She was obviously determined to make this marriage work, at least as far as the children were concerned. He thanked God again for the blessing of this woman who had been dropped into their lives.

Then Rachel raised her voice and spoke, not to Marta, but to Royce. "Pa, where's she gonna sleep?"

"She's my wife; she'll sleep with me."

"No! That's Ma's place. You can't let her sleep in Ma's place. She isn't even one of us."

Royce looked back at his oldest daughter. "She is one of us, Rachel. When the preacher said we were man and wife, Marta became a Clark. That's what it means to get married. If she doesn't sleep with me, where will she sleep? We don't have any other beds she can use."

Rachel crossed her arms over her chest. "Let her sleep in the barn."

"Rachel, she can't sleep in the barn. She isn't an animal."

Marta touched his shoulder. Then she looked at Rachel. "Where does Raeann sleep, Rachel?"

Rachel glared at her stepmother. "She sleeps in her cradle in Pa's room."

"Well then, I'll have to sleep there, too. Raeann

will need her diapers changed and food at least once during the night."

Rachel crossed her arms again. "Pa's been doing it. He don't need you to do it."

"Your pa needs to sleep, Rachel. He has to work on the ranch. Taking care of Raeann is part of what I'm supposed to be doing. So I need to sleep where she is. Now if you would prefer, I will move Raeann to your room, and I will sleep in there with you. But that means when she gets fussy in the night, she will wake you up."

"I don't want you sleeping in my room, either. Besides, I already have Rose sleeping in my room."

Marta put her finger to her lips like she was thinking. "I figure your brothers share a room, too?"

"Yes."

"Then from what I can tell, there are two people in each room. Since I need to take care of Raeann at night and there is only one person sleeping in your Pa's room, I'll just have to sleep there."

Rachel sighed and didn't say anything else all the way home. Royce hid his smile. He could see that Marta did have a plan for dealing with Rachel and he'd give her time to do so. He sighed; he'd have to make sure that Marta understood that, for now, he wouldn't require any more of her than she take care of his children and his home. Her other duties didn't actually appeal to him right now. He knew that eventually he'd want to make her his wife in truth, but Lucy's death was just too fresh right now. He couldn't even think about being intimate with anyone else.

Yet Royce knew his eyes were drawn to the curves of his new wife. She wasn't the delicate little woman his Lucy had been, but there was something about her that appealed to him. Marta was taller and a bit rounder, more full-figured with bigger hips and other womanly attributes. Almost in direct violation to the thought he'd just had, he couldn't seem to help but wonder what his new wife would be like out of those matronly, rather drab clothes she wore. He had no trouble believing she had spent her years in an orphanage and then as a nanny. She dressed just like a schoolmarm or governess. He suddenly wanted to see her in lighter, brighter dresses. Or better yet …. No, he couldn't think like that. She was here to take care of the kids and the house, not his personal needs. He loved Lucy and while Marta may look good, he wouldn't cheapen his love for his dead wife by falling for his current one. Especially when the understanding was that she was here to take care of the kids.

He was pulled out of his current thoughts by the turnoff to his ranch. He made the turn and then took a quick look over at Marta. "We're now on our land. You'll be able to see the house and barn when we top the next rise."

Marta nodded at him. "How much land do you have?"

"We have sixty-five thousand acres. But only about fifty thousand of those are grazing land. The rest is in the foothills and covered in timber. I haven't really done anything with the timber. I'm a rancher, not a lumberjack. However, Mr. Anders has discussed a partnership where he'd harvest the timber and split the profits with me. I haven't taken him up on it because I'm not sure if it would interfere with my ranching."

Marta nodded at him. "So how many cows do you have?"

Royce laughed. "Not cows, cattle. I only have one cow. She's in the barn and she's just for milk. Cattle are for beef, not milk. We have around a thousand head of cattle. I'll have a more exact count in a few months when we start the fall roundup."

"I don't know much about ranching. Is that a lot of cattle?"

Royce shook his head. "Not really, some of the

larger ranches can have up to twenty times that much. But it's enough for me. I make enough to keep my family taken care of, and that is all I really care about. I'd have to expand and purchase more land to go any bigger, and that would mean hiring more men and spending less time at home." He looked back at the kids in the back of the wagon. "That's never seemed like something I wanted to do. Maybe as the children get older. Especially as the boys get old enough to start working the ranch with me. But for now, Lucy and I made the decision that my being able to come home most nights was more important than growing the ranch."

Marta smiled at him and again his body reacted to her. "That sounds like a very good decision. I'm sure that the children are happy to have you home with them most nights."

"Yes, the only time that changes is during roundups, which happen twice a year, spring and fall. The spring roundup is when we count the new calves and make sure they're branded with the Circle C brand. Then in the fall, we round them up and decide which ones we'll drive to market. I'm gone for the cattle drive as well, and that is the longest time. It takes about a month to drive them up to Denver and sell them, then return. Roundup takes about a week. But for the most part, I'm home every evening. We sell a good amount to the mines here, too."

Marta nodded as she took in what he was saying. "How many men do you have working for you?"

Royce looked at her, trying to figure out if she was just trying to get to know him and the ranch, or if she had another motive. He really only had her word that she was heading to San Francisco to be a nanny. The rumor was that the women had all been set to go to Durango as soiled doves. What if he'd just married a Calico Queen and brought her into his house? "Why?"

She looked shocked at his question. "I'm trying to figure out what duties I'll have besides watching the children and keeping house. Will I need to cook for your ranch hands? Clean for them? Do their laundry?"

Her reasoning seemed sound, but it still left him leery. What did he really know about this woman he'd married? Nothing, that's what he knew. "I have eight men and a foreman here all year round. They have their own bunkhouse. They have a cook who sees to their food, and they deal with their individual laundry and needs. We will have more during roundups, but they are all temporary, and they also stay at the bunkhouse and take care of their own needs. So there are ten men besides me on the ranch at any time, but you won't see them all that much."

"So I don't have to worry about them. Thank you for telling me."

"I do have my foreman eat breakfast with me. It's when we talk about what needs to be done and who is going to do it that day. Will that be a problem for you?"

Marta shook her head. "Not at all. What time does that happen?"

"Five am. We start early on the ranch."

"I will make sure to have a good breakfast for the two of you by five, complete with coffee. I won't cook the children's food till later, but if it's alright with you I'll eat with you and your foreman."

"That's fine." They topped the rise, and Royce pulled the team to a stop. He motioned down below where the house, barn, bunkhouse, and chicken coop were spread out before them. "Welcome to the Circle C, Mrs. Clark."

Pride filled his voice as he welcomed her to her new home. He'd worked hard to make the place what it was, and he was proud of his ranch.

His smile grew as she gasped, "How beautiful. It's a lovely place, Royce."

"We like it."

With that, he snapped the reins and got the team heading down into the homestead. He knew she'd not be as happy when she saw the condition inside the house. It was a mess, but he'd done what he could since Lucy's death. The house would show how overwhelmed he truly had been. He just hoped she didn't demand he take her back to the Jacobs when she saw how much work there was to do. He really wouldn't be able to blame her if she did. Well, he'd know soon enough, he thought as they came to a stop. Rachel and the boys climbed down and disappeared into the house. He'd see Marta and the little ones inside, then he'd unload the supplies and get the wagon put away. At some point, he'd need to tell his hands about his new wife, but that could wait until everything else was taken care of.

Royce helped Marta down from the wagon and then picked up Rose. He followed his wife into the house. Time to see what Marta was made of.

CHAPTER 3

M arta followed Royce up to the door of the single-story ranch house. He smiled at her as he opened the door and placed his free hand on the small of her back. "Welcome home, Mrs. Clark."

That simple little statement hit her right in the heart and warmed her like a good fire on a cold winter's night. *Home*, something she'd never had. This man, as much a stranger as he still was to her, with two simple words had given her two things that she'd always wanted and never had: a family and a home. Tears fell from her eyes; she quickly wiped them before he thought she was unhappy. But she hadn't been fast enough. "Hey now, what's with the tears? I mean, I know there's a lot of work to do, but I didn't think it was anything to cry over."

She turned to him and smiled as more tears

slipped down her face. "These are happy tears. I can't tell you what your words mean to me. My whole life I've never had a home to call my own. Or a family, and you've given me both today. Thank you."

She saw him swallow as her words settled in his mind. Then he smiled again. "You might not want to thank me when you see how much work you're going to have. I'm afraid I haven't done very well at keeping the house clean or taking care of the children."

Marta moved further into the house and saw he was right. There was dirt on the floors. To the left was the parlor, which had dust over almost every surface. You could see the tracks where things had been moved around on the floors and surfaces. She looked to the right to see the dining table was covered with dishes that had been used and then stacked and pushed to the center. She sighed. Those two rooms told her what she would find in the kitchen and throughout the rest of the house. She turned back to see Royce watching her as she took everything in. She put a determined grin on her face. "I see that. I need you to go get me a clean quilt or blanket I can place Raeann on in the kitchen while I get started cleaning so we can have some dinner tonight. I don't promise a feast, but I'll find something we can have quick after I get the dishes cleaned."

"I could probably go tell the hand's cook that we need something for us to eat, and he'll send us something tonight."

While that would be the easiest thing to do, she refused to admit defeat this early in her new life. She shook her head. "I think I can handle it, but I need to get started if I'm going to have any chance. So quilt or blanket, please, unless you want to take her and Rose both and keep them busy while I get started."

Rose squirmed for her father to put her down and Marta cringed as he did, watching her totter across the dirt laden floor, leaving a trail of cleaner tracks behind her. The little girl had crawled on that floor since her mother's passing, one more day wouldn't hurt anything. But not getting some clean dishes and food on the table wouldn't endear her to her new husband or children. So first things first. She handed the baby to her father and then turned to the table. "You get her something to lie on and bring her to the kitchen, and I'll get started."

Royce nodded. "I'm sorry; I know it's a mess."

She smiled at him. "That's why you married me, Royce. Because you needed my help. I don't mind doing what is expected of me. It will be a rough couple of days, but I'll get it all under control and keep it that way. Now go and let me get to work." She grabbed two handfuls of dishes and walked through the door on the back side of the dining area into where she assumed the kitchen would be.

Sure enough, there were more dishes, pots, and pans everywhere. She shook her head and realized the first thing she needed to do was stack everything on the small table in the center of the room so that she could get a fire going in the cook stove and some water heating so she could start washing dishes.

She quickly cleaned off the stove and started a fire. Thankfully, there was a pump right in the kitchen that would save her from having to haul water from outside somewhere. She filled the water tank on the side of the stove and then filled the bucket as well and put it on top of the stove to heat. She looked through several of the pots on the stove and filled them with water to try and boil loose some of the old dried-on food and make the cleanup easier.

While the water heated, she took stock of her kitchen. There was an icebox along the inner wall; she opened it to see milk, eggs, bacon, a ham, and a small jar of butter. She decided she'd get the eggs and slice some of the ham for dinner tonight. On the other side of the kitchen, next to the door outside, was another door. She opened it to see a pantry with several tins and containers. She found coffee, tea, flour, and cornmeal. There were bottles of spices, jars of canned vegetables, and other staples. She'd make a list of what she might need tomorrow, but tonight she just grabbed a tin of lard and flour. She didn't have time to make bread, but she could make some quick biscuits. She opened the door outside to see a root cellar just passed the back of the house. She grabbed a lamp and lit it. Once she had proper light, she headed into the cellar. She grabbed an empty flour sack she found and put several potatoes in it.

Her family would have eggs, fried potatoes, ham, and biscuits for dinner tonight. That would allow her to make dinner with the least amount of clean dishes. By the time she got back into the kitchen, the water was hot. She filled the sink and quickly washed six plates, silverware for them all, and glasses. Then she tackled a Dutch oven and skillet.

She put other dishes in the hot soapy water to start soaking and quickly went out and wiped down the dining room table. She returned to the kitchen and cooked for her family. She heated a freshly cleaned and warmed bottle for Raeann and walked into the parlor where Royce had the infant. "Can you feed her this bottle while I finish fixing food for the rest of us? That way she should be sleeping while we are all eating."

He took the bottle and smiled at her. "Thank you, Marta. I'm sure this isn't how you planned to spend your wedding day."

She smiled back at him. "Honestly, I never had any plans for a wedding day. I was on my way to become a nanny, remember? If you hadn't asked me to marry you, I'd never have gotten married."

"I find that hard to believe. I'm sure some gentleman out in San Francisco would have caught your attention, and you'd have ended up married with a family."

She shook her head. "Doubtful; most single men of good character don't notice the help of their married friends. Those that do notice don't want marriage. They want a mistress or a fling. I wasn't willing to be either. I'd honestly determined that being a spinster who took care of other's children was my lot in life."

Royce smiled up at her. "Then I'm glad you happened to come by the mercantile when you did. I got the wife I needed, and you have a home and family. I'd say God must have been looking out for both of us today."

Marta thought about that and knew it was true. After all, it was an angel, or at least a woman who claimed to be an angel, who sent her to the mercantile at that exact time.

She just nodded and agreed with Royce. No sense telling him an angel sent her to him. He might think she was unbalanced. She wasn't completely sure she hadn't gone insane for a short time after getting that letter. After all, why would God send her an angel? It wasn't like she was anyone important. Just Marta Campbell, now Clark. Campbell wasn't even her real name, just one the Mother Superior chose for her. She wasn't anyone; while her last name had changed, she knew, in reality, she was still the help. Royce was obviously still in love with his children's mother. He only married her out of desperation. Hers was nothing more than a marriage of convenience. But it still gave her a home and a family, and for that, she would be eternally thankful to him, even if love was never going to be part of her life. She'd come to accept that already anyway. Today didn't change that one bit.

She turned and headed back to the kitchen. She'd get dinner ready and feed the family, and then get back to work setting the kitchen to rights. After that, she'd go through the house and start figuring out what to do next. She may not have love, but she would make herself indispensable to him. He may never love her, but he'd realize quickly enough he couldn't live without her. That would be sufficient for her.

~

Marta quickly got the ham cooked along with the eggs, potatoes, and biscuits. As her new family sat at the table together and ate her simple meal like they'd not had food in a month, she couldn't help but smile. They reminded her so much of the kids at the orphanage. Hunkered down over their food, shoveling it into their mouths like it was going to disappear if they didn't get it inside their bellies right now. "Slow down or you'll all give yourselves a bellyache."

She could see Royce physically force himself to slow down. "It's just *so* good!"

Marta blushed at the praise. "It's just eggs, ham, and potatoes; it's not like it was something hard to fix."

RJ grinned up at her, "But it ain't beans and burned bacon. I'm so tired of beans and bacon. I hope you never fix them for us."

Marta smiled at RJ as Randy and even Rachel nodded. "I promise that I won't make any beans for a while, and I won't burn the bacon. I will make sure that you have three good meals a day. Starting tomorrow, I'll see about having something sweet for dessert, too."

The boy's eyes went big. "You can make sweets?"

Marta laughed. "Well, if you think cookies and cakes and pies are sweets, then yes, I can make sweets."

"Did you hear that Pa? She's going to make us sweets."

Royce smiled at her. "I did hear that. What do you say to her for being so thoughtful?"

RJ looked at his pa for a minute confused, and then she saw when it dawned on him what his pa wanted him to say. "Thank You."

She smiled at him. "You are welcome, RJ. Now we need to figure something out here. I don't want you to keep calling me she all the time. What are you all going to call me?"

They all looked at Royce as if to leave the decision up to him, but before he could open his mouth

Rachel spoke up. "Well, I don't care what we call you, but I ain't calling you Ma because I already have a ma, and you ain't her."

"Rachel!" Royce gave her a disapproving look.

Marta reached out a hand to Rachel. "No, you're right Rachel, you shouldn't call me Ma. You had a ma who loved you very much, and I don't want to be called by the same name you called her." Marta looked around and saw that all of them were sad again. "Rachel, will you help me carry everyone's dishes into the kitchen, and then we can wash them so they'll be ready to use for breakfast."

Rachel huffed, but a look from Royce had her slowly getting to her feet and gathering plates. Together they took the dishes into the kitchen. Marta stood between Rachel and the door back to the dining room. "Rachel, I don't want you to call me Ma, and I don't want you to forget your ma. I know you think I'm going to take her place, but I'm not. I'm going to help take care of your pa and your family, but I'm not going to take your ma's place. I'm going to make my own place in your family."

The little girl's arms crossed over her chest again. "We don't need you in our family."

Marta knelt down on the girl's level. "We both know that isn't true, Rachel. I'm sure that your ma taught you lots of things, and I'm sure you think you can take care of your family alone, but we both know that isn't true, don't we?"

"It is too true!"

Marta shook her head. "Oh, little one, we both know it isn't. I don't think your ma would be happy with how the house looks, would she? But you can't do it all yourself. Your ma didn't do it all herself. She had you to help her. Now I'm here, and I'll help you. Together we can take care of our family. I can't do it all alone, either. I'll need your help just like your ma did. So I make you a promise. You help me with taking care of our family, and I'll help you make sure your brothers, and sisters always remember your ma."

The little girl looked at her with surprise on her face. "What do you mean?"

"I mean every night we will sit with your brothers and sisters, and you can tell them a story about your ma and the things she did. It may take a while, but after your pa is done feeling sad, he will probably help you tell stories about her."

The girl wiped at the tears on her face. "You mean it? You won't try to make us forget Ma?"

She reached out and pulled the little girl into her arms. "Oh, Rachel, of course not. Without her, I wouldn't have you as part of my new family or your brothers or sisters. I will always be happy to hear you talk about her. But you have to let me help you take care of our family, okay?"

The little girl grabbed hold of her and wrapped her arms around her neck. "I miss her so much. Why did God have to take her from me?"

"Oh, honey, God didn't take her from you. She was just too sick to get better. But I'm sure she is looking down at you from heaven. She must be so proud of you for trying to take care of your pa and family. Maybe she sent me to help you. Did you think of that?"

The little girl looked up at her. "You think so?"

"I don't know, honey, but I know this. You just happened to be in the street when I happened to walk by. So who knows? Now, let's get these dishes done and then you can show me the rest of the house. Because tomorrow we have to start getting it clean again."

The little girl smiled and pulled a smaller apron off of a hook by the door and put it on over her clothes. She handed Marta a larger one hanging beside it. But when Marta tried it on, she couldn't tie it around her. It seems she was a bit bigger in the hips than the last Mrs. Clark was. "I think I need to go get my own apron, Rachel."

Rachel giggled, and Marta took off the apron and hung it back on the peg she'd taken it from. "Let me see if your Pa brought my trunk in yet. I have a couple of aprons in it. Would you like to come with me and help me look?"

"Okay."

They went back into the main parlor where Royce was changing Rose. "We're almost out of diapers for the little ones."

"Rachel and I will wash those first tomorrow, then. Have you brought my trunk in yet?"

"I did; it's in our room. Why?"

"Well, it seems that I need to get an apron from it. The one Rachel gave me to use was a bit... tight."

"Let me show you where our room is."

"That's not necessary. Rachel and I need to look at the house anyway. She will show me. That way we women of the house can make a plan to get things under control." She winked at her husband, hoping he'd understand what she was doing. He looked back and forth between the two of them. "Is that okay with you, Rachel?"

The little girl nodded. "Of course, Pa; that's what us womenfolk are supposed to do, isn't it?"

Marta swallowed the giggle that threatened to escape at the surprised look on Royce's face. "Yes, I suppose it is. Carry on then."

The two of them walked through. Rachel pointed out the different rooms and Marta showed her the things that they'd need to do to get the house back to normal. She pulled an apron out of her trunk and put it on. Afterward, she and the girl went back to the kitchen and washed all the dishes that had soaked, as well as the dinner dishes. Then they went into the parlor with the rest of the family, sat together on the divan, and made a list of the things they would start cleaning tomorrow. Marta pointed out that they'd work down the list and that it was okay if it took them more than one day to do everything. Before long, the children were all yawning and Marta suggested that everyone get ready for bed. She let Rachel help her put the younger kids to bed, and she shared something with each of them about their ma. Then she let Marta tuck her in as well. "Maybe it won't be so bad to have you as part of our family."

Marta's heart squeezed in her chest. "Thank you, Rachel. That means a lot to me. Good night, sleep sweet."

The little girl smiled at her. "My ma used to say that to me."

"Well, tonight I'll say it for both of us. Sleep sweet, Rachel."

"Sleep sweet, Marta"

Marta left the room and went back in the parlor where Royce was. He looked at her like she was a wonder. "How in the world did you get Rachel on your side so quickly?"

"I just assured her that I wasn't trying to make her or your family forget her mother. I promised if she helped me take care of the family, I would help her make sure everyone remembered her Ma."

Royce's face looked pained. "Are you sure that's a good idea?"

"Royce, they need to remember their mother. Just because she is gone doesn't mean they need to pretend she didn't exist. Yes, it will bring some tears sometimes, but it will help them heal. It will help you as well."

"I don't want to think about her right now."

"I understand, Royce. You miss her, and you still love her. That's okay. I'm tired; would it be all right if I go on to bed?"

"Sure, how long do you need to get ready?"

She shrugged. "Ten minutes?"

"All right. I sleep on the right side if that's okay with you."

"That's fine. I can sleep in here if that would be better for you."

He shook his head. "No, if you're going to take care of the baby, then you need to be where she is. We'll make it work."

"Okay, then good night." Marta went and quickly changed and checked on Raeann who was still asleep. She climbed into bed on the left side and had just gotten settled when Royce came in. She stayed facing away as he quickly got ready for bed and slid in beside her. He turned out the lantern; she laid there listening to him breathe until she finally fell into an exhausted sleep.

CHAPTER 4

R oyce woke to a warm body pressed up against him. His arm was around his wife; he pulled her tight against him, reveling in the feel of her body against his. His hand had moved to caress her curves when he realized that this wasn't his Lucy, it was his new wife, Marta. He quickly pulled his hand away and flew from the bed.

He pulled on his pants from the night before, grabbed the least dirty shirt, and quickly exited the room. He needed to do something, anything, to get his body under control. In his not quite awake and aware state, he had responded to the curves pressed against him in the most natural way. He'd almost betrayed the memory of his love for Lucy. He needed to be more careful.

He finished dressing and went to the kitchen to

start a fire in the stove and put on coffee. Then he went and filled the wood bucket so that Marta would have it when she got up. He'd go and take care of the early morning chores. Anything to give his body time to settle down before he had to face Marta this morning. He just prayed that she'd still been asleep and hadn't realized what he'd almost done. How could his body betray him like that? He loved Lucy and had only been attracted to her for so long that he was a bit overwhelmed by the way he seemed to react to Marta.

Royce sat and began to milk the cow, but his thoughts strayed again to his lovely new wife and how perfect it had felt to hold her tight. He groaned in frustration. He wasn't supposed to be attracted to her. He married her to take care of the house and children. Lucy was the love of his life; she had been since he was old enough to know the difference between boys and girls. While he may have the right to Marta and intimacy with her, he didn't know her well enough yet. Even when they got to know each other he didn't plan to take his rights often, only when need demanded. She wasn't his wife for love, just to provide security for her and a helping hand with his domestic life for him.

He took the milk bucket, sat it on the table in the

kitchen, and grabbed the basket to gather eggs. He entered the chicken enclosure and threw out some feed for the fowl, then entered the hen house and gathered the eggs while trying to sort out his thoughts and feelings for his new wife. Why had his body betrayed him like it had this morning? Was it just a physical response to the close proximity and lack of proper attire? Or was there something about Marta herself that had caused his reaction? It had to be nothing more than a remembered action; something that he and Lucy had done hundreds of times. Yes, that was what happened. His body wasn't actually reacting to Marta; it was reacting to a warm female in his arms just like it had when Lucy was still the one in his arms and in his bed. With that thought, he was able to put the nagging thought that he wasn't being honest with himself to rest. He'd just have to train himself not to react like that anymore. Nothing to it. Now that Marta was here, he could get back to ranching and work long and hard until he collapsed with exhaustion at night.

He carried the eggs into the kitchen and stopped at the door. Marta was at the table mixing up bread or biscuits; he didn't know which. She was once again dressed in the drab tan dress she had worn when he first met her in town. She had a dark gray apron on over it to protect the dress. She looked the perfect example of a governess or nanny. But that wasn't what stopped Royce in his tracks. It was the way her whole body seemed to be moving as she mixed the dough. While the dress may be dull to keep people from focusing on her, the way her perfect curves were dancing as she worked had Royce taking notice in ways he'd just convinced himself he wouldn't.

He quickly moved to the table so that he could hide the effect her movements had on him. "Good morning."

She blushed when she looked at him. He grimaced; she'd been awake, then, when he'd pawed her this morning. Royce cleared his throat. "Umm... about this morning...I apologize. I umm...wasn't quite awake and my body reacted the way it used to with Lucy."

Marta blushed again and bit her bottom lip. That did nothing but make him want to pull her into his arms again and nibble on it himself. She finally sighed and answered him. "You have nothing to apologize for. You're my husband and if you want to hold me and, umm, touch me, then you have every right to do so."

He swallowed at the images her statement caused

to fly through his mind. "That may be true, but that wasn't the reason I married you. We agreed that you would become my wife to take care of my home and children, not my umm...physical needs. I assure you I am not the type of man to force my attentions on any woman, wife or not."

She smiled shyly and nodded. "Then your apology is accepted. However, I must point out that we both know there will come a time when you will need to become more physical in our interactions. It is, after all, the way God created us."

Royce wanted to tell her that she was wrong, but they both were old enough to know that she was right. "That is probably true. However, right now that is not necessary."

She bit her lip again. "That was not what I was trying to say. I would appreciate it if we at least got to know each other a bit better before that point."

Royce's eyebrows dipped in concentration and confusion. "What did you have in mind?"

"It would be appreciated if we were to ease into more physical encounters."

"How do you suggest we do that?"

"Well, I was thinking that before you get to the point that you need me to fulfill all my wifely duties, it might be best if I got used to any kind of intimacy with you. For example, the only kiss we've shared was a very quick and chaste one at our wedding."

He grinned knowing that now he could tease her. "Why, Mrs. Clark, are you asking me to kiss you properly?"

Marta blushed again and then straightened herself and nodded one single time. "I think it would be a good first step, don't you?"

"I reckon it might at that." Royce moved slowly, like a mountain lion stalking its prey, around the table to stand beside Marta who was kneading the dough as hard and fast as she could. He reached down and took her hands in his, turned her to face him, and looked into her whiskey-colored eyes, realizing that while they were mostly a light smoky-brown, there were starbursts of gold around the irises. "Your eyes are very pretty, Marta. Has anyone told you that before?"

She swallowed and shook her head. "I told you no one notices the help."

His head moved closer to hers as he released her hands and moved to hold the back of her neck, drawing her ever closer as his eyes dropped to her full lips. "That's their loss, Marta." His voice had gone husky and breathless and before she could say anything, his lips claimed her. She stiffened for a moment as contact was made and then she relaxed and her arms came up around his neck. Her mouth responded to his and unexpectedly he felt a physical jolt as desire for this woman slammed fresh through his body. His kiss, which had been slightly less chaste than the one he'd given her at their wedding, quickly climbed to hungry, and he was passionately claiming her mouth with his own. She melted against him and his hand tightened around the short hairs at the back of her neck. She responded to the level of passion he was pouring into her, and he realized that he wanted his wife. That thought shocked him and he pulled back. He stepped away from her. What was he doing? Lucy wasn't even three months in her grave, and he was devouring another woman's mouth like his life depended on it.

He took another step away from her and turned before heading out of the kitchen. He pretended not to see the look of disappointment that crossed Marta's face. He threw his statement back over his shoulder as he went out the door, "I've got work to see to before breakfast." Then he all but fled. Now what was he going to do? He couldn't deny the attraction that kiss had exposed; next best thing was to ignore it and pray that he'd be able to forget how perfect her lips had felt against his. How well her body had fitted his.

He stalked into the barn. He'd turn out the horses and start mucking the stalls even though that was part of his three wranglers' jobs. However, today he'd do it because physical work was what he needed. That and as much time away from Marta Clark as he could reasonably make happen.

~

Marta watched as Royce stormed out of the house like his shirt tail was on fire. She couldn't stop her hand from going to her lips. Nothing she'd ever experienced or even heard about had prepared her for the reality of her first 'real' kiss. The tingle that had started in her lips as he pressed his against hers had grown until it was a raging inferno running through her body as he'd responded to her acceptance of his lips. She didn't know what he must think of her, but all she could do was hold on tight to him as her legs had turned to water. She'd leaned heavily on him, not wanting the feeling to ever end. All too soon, he'd pulled away. She wanted to yank him back against her, but she couldn't even think of how to do so. Then he'd turned and all but run away from her.

What had she done that had caused him to pull away? Was she bad at kissing? Maybe she'd been too wanton. It was times like this she wished she'd grown up with a mother instead of in an orphanage with a bunch of nuns. She didn't even have a friend who she could ask what she'd done wrong. A single tear slipped out of her eye and raced down her face. She wiped it and turned back to her bread dough. She quickly divided it and sat it on the windowsill to rise. She began to make a batter for pancakes. She'd not worry about it. Maybe if she fed him and got the house under control today, he'd kiss her again before they went to bed.

She set the batter to the side, grabbed bacon, and sliced several strips. She knew that Royce said his foreman would join them for breakfast. She'd make the best breakfast she could for them and prove he hadn't made a mistake marrying her. She'd do whatever she needed to so that he'd want to keep her around. Having tasted him, she couldn't even think of not feeling his lips on hers again. Or his strong hands on her waist and at the back of her head. She'd felt so small and dainty. Something she knew she wasn't, but he'd made her feel that way and she wanted that feeling again.

She remembered seeing some dried apples in the root cellar and hurried down to grab some. She mixed some water and sugar in a pan with the apples and set them on a less hot part of the stove. She'd make an apple syrup to put on the pancakes since she didn't see any maple syrup in the pantry. Then she started making the pancakes. She'd make sure both men had their fill of good food this morning. As she went about her task of preparing breakfast, she was mentally running over the list she and Rachel had made last night. She had water heating for laundry already. Once she'd fed the men, she'd start on the diapers she'd need for both the younger children. She could probably have them on the line drying before she'd have to get the children up for their breakfast. Dishes could wait till the children were finished eating; she'd have Rachel help her with those.

She had pulled the last of the pancakes off the stove, put a plate stacked high with them and a platter of bacon on the table when the front door opened and Royce came in with a slightly shorter older man in a well-worn pair of jeans and canvas shirt behind him. Had she not known the man was a cowboy, she would have thought he was a trapper or mountain man: his hair was sticking up every way and he sported a bushy, wild beard and mustache. Royce smiled at her and motioned to the man beside him. "Marta, this is Fuzzy Knight, my foreman. Fuzzy, my new wife, Marta."

The older cowboy nodded to her. "Howdy, ma'am. I'm right pleased ta know ya. Reckon Royce here wouldn't a made it many more days iffen he hadn't found ya. Them young'uns are his pride and joy but he ain't no good as a ma."

Marta smiled at the older cowboy. "Yes, that was very obvious when I arrived yesterday, Mr. Knight."

The ranch hand laughed, and it brought thoughts of Jolly ole Saint Nick to Marta's mind. "It's jest Fuzzy, ma'am. Ain't no one ever accused me of being fancy enough to be called mister anything."

"Well, Fuzzy, thank you for your warm welcome. You and Royce come and eat before your food gets cold."

The two men sat at the table and began to fill their plates. Marta grabbed the coffee pot and filled their cups for them. Then she sat at the end of the table and filled her own plate as she listened to the two talk about what jobs they'd assign to each hand that day. They also talked about the rumor that some of their competitors had encountered rustlers.

"I'm thinkin' we should start having a couple of the men riding guard on the herd at night, boss."

Royce scratched his chin where his own beard was starting to get a bit wild. "I don't know, Fuzzy. We don't have any solid word of rustlers, just a couple of saloon rumors. I'll ride over to talk to Jeffers later today. If he confirms the rumors, then maybe. I just hate to put more work on the boys."

"I understand. I'm gonna have Slim and Buster bring the remuda in tonight and put 'em in the barn. As much as I'd hate to lose beeves, losing them horses would be worse."

Royce nodded, "I agree. I don't want to lose cattle but it would be devastating to lose them horses. I'd have to either have Otto train more, or send a wire to Nathan Ryder or that new guy he told us about last time he was up here. What was his name? The rancher in Montana?"

Fuzzy thought for a minute, "Williams, weren't it? Bought a bunch of mustangs offa Nugget Nate before he passed on. Was gonna train them to be cow ponies, weren't he?"

Royce nodded, "Yep that was him. Still, can't figure that would be cheap."

"Reckon not." Fuzzy turned his attention back to Marta. "These here are some mighty tasty vittles, Mrs. Clark. Ain't never had a fluffier skillet cake. And that there topping is about the best thing I ever done put in my mouth."

Marta smiled at him "Thank you, Fuzzy. I'm glad you're enjoying them."

"Boss, we should introduce yer bride to the boys afore they ride out today. That way they'll know ta keep an eye out fer her iffen they're close by."

Royce nodded, "Probably a good idea." He looked at Marta. "What was your plan today?"

She thought for a minute. "I'm going to start on laundry and giving the house a good scrubbing. I'll probably go through the pantry and root cellar and see what, if any, supplies I need. I also need to look at the children's clothes and see what needs to be mended or let out as well."

"Well, I don't want you or the children leaving the ranch without an escort. While things have been a bit better since Archie was arrested, there are still too many men without scruples around for me to feel safe letting you all go anywhere alone."

Marta wanted to protest but she thought about how easy it had been for Dougal to grab her and whisk her away without anyone the wiser. She

RESCUING THE RANCHER   59

nodded her acceptance. "That's fine. We'll be sticking around here today. I may take them all out for a walk after lunch, but we will stay on the ranch."

"Even then, I want you to let one of the men know where you're going and which direction. It's dangerous out here, too."

Marta nodded. She wondered, though, if he was worried about her safety or that of his children. *Did it really matter,* she asked herself and was surprised to find that the answer was yes, it did matter because she was already beginning to develop feelings for this broken, heartsick family and especially her husband.

CHAPTER 5

Royce was checking the fence along his eastern border. He had asked Fuzzy to send a hand to check each section. With the rumors of rustlers in the area, he wanted to make sure that the newfangled barbwire was doing its job and keeping his cattle where he put them. The job didn't take a whole lot of thought, just riding and stopping on occasion to check that the posts were still solid and the wire was still tight, allowing his thoughts to turn to the situation he now found himself in. He could tell his new wife wasn't happy being stuck on the ranch and not even being able to go for a walk around the property without letting someone know where they were. She needed to realize that this wasn't back East where she'd worked as a nanny or even San Francisco where things were a bit more civilized. This was Colorado and it was still untamed; even if it wasn't for the rumors of rustlers, there were still plenty of other dangers to a person's life. Why, he still remembered the mountain lion pelt that Hugh Fontaine had shown around claiming the woman he married killed it with an umbrella. He didn't know if he believed that's what killed it but there was no denying that big cats were a part of the landscape. While he wouldn't let himself fall in love with Marta, that didn't mean he wanted to see her hurt or killed.

He thought again about what he was going to do about his physical reactions to Marta. She had every right to expect him to get to know her and show affection toward her. She was also right that eventually his physical needs would necessitate him making her his wife in every way. So he did need to make the effort to spend time with her, kissing her, and letting her get comfortable with him. However, it felt like a betrayal of his love for Lucy. It felt wrong, like he was cheating on her. He turned and kicked Blue into a trot. He needed to go spend some time with Lucy and see if he could resolve this issue. Then he still needed to ride over to the Morgan ranch and see what Waylon knew about the rumors his hands had heard about rustlers.

Soon enough, Royce pulled up just outside the small area he'd set aside when it came time to bury Lucy. It was a patch of ground big enough for a few more graves. He could have buried her in the graveyard beside the church in Creede, but it just felt right to keep her here on the ranch. This way, when he or the kids needed to, they could come out and visit with her just like he was doing now.

He tied Blue to the fence post outside the little graveyard and walked over to the small stone he'd carved and chiseled Lucy's name and date on. He knelt down, running his fingers along her name and then letting his hand linger over it. "Sorry it's been a few days since I got out here to talk to ya, Lucy. I sure miss ya, honey. Reckon you know I got married. I didn't want to and she doesn't mean anything to me, but I needed help with the kids and the house.

"Her name's Marta and she was one of them women who went missing right before you gave birth. She was on her way to California to be a nanny when that no account Dougal snatched her from the street for Archie's saloon up in Durango. She seems like a nice enough lady. She sure knows how to cook and how to get the young'uns to mind.

Rachel was a bit rude to her at first, but Marta sorted her right out. The boys seem to like her, and I got the first good night's sleep since you left me.

"I don't know what to do, Lucy. Marta is a good woman; she deserves a husband who can give her his heart and bring her the happiness we had together. I just can't do it. I feel like I'm cheating on you with every kiss she asks for." He hurried on with the next part, "Not that there've been a lot of them. However, she wants to get comfortable with a physical relationship. I'm sure you saw what happened this morning. I don't know how to keep that from happening again. You know how much I used to like holding you in the morning. I just don't know what to do. If it weren't so close to roundup and the cattle drive I'd build another room on the house, but with the fire in Creede and roundup just a month away, I'm not sure we'd be able to get any lumber or have the time to build."

Royce pulled his bandana out of his back pocket and wiped his face. "What do you think I should do, Lucy? How do I guard my heart and stay faithful to you while fulfilling my obligations to Marta?"

Royce jerked upright when he was answered, "You do know she ain't gonna answer ya, don't cha?"

Royce looked to see a man with sandy hair and

the wildest expanse of facial hair he'd ever seen sitting on top of the split-rail fence directly in front of Lucy's headstone.

"Who are you, and how did you get here?" Royce demanded. The second part of the question was the most important because the buckskin and moccasin clad stranger had no horse or mule that Royce could see. He looked like a trapper or a mountain man, but he couldn't have walked up without Royce noticing something.

"Not sure you could say my real name so why don't you jest call me Daniel. I knew a feller once called that who was a mighty wise feller so I'll just use that name fer now. As to how I got here that ain't important. I go where the Boss sends me."

Royce was not happy with that answer. "Well, why did your boss send you to my wife's graveside?"

The stranger lifted his coonskin cap and scratched his head. "He didn't send me to this grave-side. He sent me to you, Royce Clark. Told me ta give ya a message."

"How did your boss know to send you to me here? And what message?"

The mountain man shook his head. "Not my boss, the Boss." He looked and pointed up. "You know the Boss of all bosses, King of all kings, Lord of all lords. The BOSS."

Royce took a step back. "You're saying that God told you to bring me a message?"

Daniel smiled. "Of course, He told me to bring ya a message; I'm a messenger, ain't I?"

"You're a messenger? Like an angel?"

"I knew ya'd figure it out. Now listen, you is thinking about yer situation with yer wife all wrong."

Royce wasn't sure this buckskin-clad person was in his right mind and didn't know what to do to end this conversation and get the man off his ranch. The man stopped talking and glared at Royce. "I ain't crazy. We come to you people in a form you can understand. It never went so good when we showed up in our real forms. Ain't cha ever wondered why every angel in the Bible says don't be afraid?"

"No, I can't say that I have."

The man sighed. "I can see yer gonna be a tough one. Fine; I'll let ya see, but remember I warned ya."

Then a light seemed to start shining from the man's center, and it got brighter with every second until Royce couldn't deny what was happening. The light flared and for just a brief moment Royce saw the vision of the angel unhindered by the form of the trapper. He saw the wings and eyes and visage of the holy messenger in its natural form. Just as the angel had tried to explain, it did fill Royce with a type of reverent fear. Then the light blazed so bright that Royce covered his face. When he removed his hands, the mountain man stood before him again. "Ya convinced now?"

Royce swallowed hard. "Yes, I believe that you are an angel. You said you had a message for me?"

The angel, Daniel, nodded. "Yes. The message was this; yer holding on to Lucy but she ain't there." Daniel pointed to the grave. "She is in glory with the Creator. It's time ya let her go."

Royce shook his head "I can't. I made a vow to her before God to love her, to be faithful to her."

The messenger nodded his head. "That's right, you did, but yer forgetting part of that vow, ain't ya? That vow was until death, and Lucy is dead. Ya fulfilled yer vow."

"You make it sound easy."

"I never said it would be easy, but I just give the message. Think on this, Royce Clark; you made those same vows to Marta. You ain't keeping them."

Royce felt anger rising up inside him. "That's not fair. I didn't have a choice. I needed Marta's help. She understands that I don't love her."

The angel just stared at him. Royce stood defiantly but with every passing second, he felt more uncomfortable. Then Daniel spoke. "Time of choice is comin' ta ya, Royce Clark. It's comin' fast."

Royce was confused. This conversation seemed to have changed, and he didn't understand why. "What's that got to do with Marta?"

The angel straightened. "It has everything to do with Marta and with you. What reason do you have to hold on to the past? Why would you not embrace the woman the Boss sent to you in your hour of need?"

Royce looked down at the tombstone and knelt once more to stroke the name he had chiseled into the stone. How did he explain to anyone how his heart wanted things to be different? How he married Marta because he knew his children needed her. He couldn't and wouldn't let himself need her beyond what he had to.

Daniel spoke from behind him. "Soon you will have to choose to let go of the past. To let go of a vow that you've already fulfilled and move forward to keep the vow you made to your current wife; or you could choose to hold on to your past, the vows you refuse to see as fulfilled. In choosing the second one, you'll lose the future the Boss has planned for you. Choose well, Royce Clark, for your choice will affect not only you and your wife but your children and their futures as well."

"What do you mean by that?" Royce demanded as he quickly stood and turned to confront the angel. Only there was no one there. If he'd had any doubt that the mountain man was an angel as he claimed, he didn't now. He wondered what the messenger had meant by his last statement. He shuddered as he considered the words again. The whole last statement had the feeling of a warning. He walked over to Blue and climbed into the saddle. Dire warnings aside, he had rumors to run down. He'd head home for lunch and then ride over to the Morgan Ranch and talk to Waylon. Afterward, he'd head into Creede and talk with the sheriff and see if there are any truth to the rumors. He turned Blue toward the ranch house and some of Marta's cooking. He may not let his heart love her, but he would enjoy her skills in the kitchen for certain sure.

~

Marta's day had been hectic so far. After she'd been introduced to the men who lived at the ranch, she had watched as Royce had saddled his horse, Blue, and rode out to work on checking fences. He'd told her he'd be back for lunch with her and the children. She went to the kitchen and cleaned up the dishes she'd used to feed Royce and Fuzzy. She'd stuck a plate of food in the oven to stay warm until she got the children up.

She quickly gathered the sheets off the bed she and Royce had slept in, and all the used diapers, and both Rose and Raeann's soakers and took them to the washroom she had found attached to the back of the house. Rachel told Marta that Royce had built it for Lucy the year before when she complained how hard it was to be pregnant and do the laundry outside in the cold. The room had two enormous tubs, one for washing, and one for rinsing. There was a wringer attached to the rinse tub. There was a small stove and two large buckets for heating water. Clotheslines were strung to hang the clothing on in the cold weather so that the heat from the stove would help them dry.

Marta washed the linens and baby things. She

hung them on the line strung outside since it was only mid-July and warm outside. She put some more water on to heat. She would do all the linens and have the children gather up the rest of the laundry. She'd do some more tomorrow morning. She went inside to wake the children and get them fed. She put the bottle for Raeann in a pot of water to warm as she woke everyone.

Marta had done everything with thoughts of Royce's kisses and questioning why he'd pulled back so suddenly filling her head. She knew that he was attracted to her; it would have been impossible for her not to know that after the way he'd held her this morning in the bed. However, just like the kisses she asked for afterward, he jumped away from her like he couldn't make up his mind if he was going to allow himself to be her husband or not. She wondered if it was just that he was still grieving the loss of his first wife or was it that he didn't find her as attractive as Lucy. Marta knew she was a bit bigger than what most men were attracted to. She also had more drab, don't-pay-attention-to-me clothes than pretty dresses and gowns. Before that had never bothered her. However, now that she was married to a man who made her heart race when she saw him, she wanted his to race at the thought of her, too. Had she condemned herself to a life without love? It wasn't so bad when you were single to know you wouldn't be the person who put that look on someone's face. It was another thing when you had a husband and still didn't seem to be able to evoke passion and adoration. Maybe she shouldn't have listened to that stupid angel.

She shook that thought from her head. This family needed her and even if that was all she ever had, it would be enough. She got Rachel up and asked her to get Rose changed and dressed while she went and woke her brothers. Once all the older children were dressed and at the table eating, she got Raeann up and changed her. Afterwards, Marta sat with the children as she fed the baby. "All right, today we are going to spend time playing the treasure hunt game."

Randy looked up at her, his blue eyes wide. "What's that?"

Marta smiled at him. "I'm so glad you asked me, Randy. Today I'm going to give you a list of things I need you to find for me here at the house. When you find them, you'll bring them to me and I'll give you a point for each one. Whoever has the most points by the end of the game will get their dessert at dinner served first."

RJ looked at her like he knew this was a trick of some kind. "What kind of things are you going to send us to find?"

"You'll just have to wait and see, RJ. But I promise you I'm not going to make it easy for you to find the things I want."

"What if I don't want to play your game? I want to go out and help Slim with the horses."

Marta looked at the older boy. "RJ, I understand that you want to go help with the ranch work; I will talk with your pa when he comes home for lunch to see if that's okay with him. Until then, I need you to stay with me and help out with our game."

The boy's face showed he wasn't happy about this situation, but he knew his pa had told them they had to listen to Marta just like they'd listened to their ma. So he huffed and finished his food. Once they were all done, Marta told them they needed to help her with her treasure hunt by finding her the dirtiest pair of pants they could. She told RJ and Randy they could only bring her pants that belonged to themselves. She told Rachel she could bring in their pa's since she didn't have any pants.

That's how the morning went with Marta having the kids compete with each other in helping her sort the laundry and gather the things that needed to be cleaned. By the time Royce rode up to have lunch with them, the laundry was mostly done and drying on the line, and Marta had found how much the older three knew school-wise. She wanted to talk to Royce after they went to bed tonight about the possibility of getting them into the school in Bachelor that her friend Julianne Fontaine had started. She figured it would be too far for them to travel daily, but maybe she could get together with Julianne once a week, get the next week's lessons from her, and go over them with the children here at the ranch. She knew how important it was for them to know how to read, write, and work their sums.

Lunch went well except for the fact that Marta felt like Royce was there but avoiding her. He had given permission for the older three to play outside, either between the ranch house, bunkhouse, and barn, or out back between the laundry and the house where Marta could see them. Then, with only a quick kiss, he was gone. He'd told Marta that he needed to ride into Creede and over to see one of the neighbors about some rumors of ranches being hit by rustlers and other trouble.

She hoped that he just had a lot on his mind and that she hadn't done something to make him decide she wasn't worth paying attention to. She didn't expect him to fall in love with her but, for the most part, he wasn't even acknowledging her. This was not what she'd wanted in a marriage. She'd have been better off to have found another nanny position than the way things were now.

CHAPTER 6

Royce was headed southwest toward Topaz. He knew he'd reach Waylon's ranch before he got to the little town. He didn't spend much time in Topaz; no one did, it just wasn't much of a town, even less than Creede. He knew that Waylon's men would have gone to Creede if they were looking forward to blowing off a little steam. Hopefully, they had heard more information than the rumors his hands had heard. Maybe Waylon had heard some-thing more definite about what might be going on than just a few rumors passed among drunk cowboys and miners.

Royce noticed a rider headed his way. He pulled his Winchester from its saddle boot and set it across the saddle. This was still Creede after all, and while he'd be friendly, he'd also be smart.

Desperate men sometimes did desperate things and since the fire last month some men had to be very desperate. As he got closer, he relaxed and slid the rifle back in the saddle boot. He noticed his neighbor do the same thing. "Clark, didn't expect to see you today. Heard a rumor you got married yesterday."

"Not a rumor; I married one of the women who had gone missing. Marta Campbell was her name. She was going to California to be a nanny. When she didn't show up, they replaced her. Since I need help with my children and the woman-work around the ranch, seemed like a good fit for both of us."

"Shouldn't you be home getting to know the little woman?"

Royce shook his head. "Isn't like that, Morgan. My heart belongs to Lucy; you know that. Marta's fine with the arrangement we have." Royce felt a little guilty about that statement because he knew it wasn't exactly true. The words of the messenger came to his mind again and he pushed them away. "Besides, I needed to find out the truth about these rustler rumors. That's why I was headed to your ranch. I figured if anyone knew the truth, it would be you."

Morgan's face hardened. "They aren't rumors,

and it isn't just rustlers. It seems someone is trying to push the little ranchers out of the area."

Royce's heart sped up at that declaration. He'd heard of the types of techniques bigger ranchers sometimes used to push the little guy out of the area. None of them was good and they often led to a range war. That was something Creede didn't need. "Do we know who?"

"No, but a couple of the smaller ranches closer to Topaz had a guy in a suit show up last few weeks offering to buy their spreads and cattle. Price was always a bit too low to make it worthwhile. Then suddenly they have cattle missing. Jefferson had several hands up and quit. All of them looking like they'd taken a beating before they left. He thinks someone encouraged them to move on. Then last night Andrew's bunkhouse and barn were torched. While he and the hands were fighting the fire, his whole herd was stolen. That's why I was heading to Creede; I need to see whether the sheriff will take this seriously now and start investigating."

Royce was shocked. He didn't know all this was going on. "You mean the sheriff knows about this?"

Morgan nodded as they started riding toward Creede. "Yeah, he knows about the rumors, as he called them the last time we talked. Said there weren't enough lawmen to hunt down rustlers. He indicated that we ranchers should deal with it ourselves. He also suggested that the little guys take the offers to sell they were being given."

Royce looked at the other rancher. "You think he's in on it?"

Morgan shrugged. "Don't know. Everyone knows he doesn't do anything without Anders say so. It just struck me as strange that he knew about the offers to buy them ranches. I didn't think Anders was interested in ranching. He's always been willing to buy his beef from us ranchers."

Royce grunted and thought about that. "If Archie wasn't in jail, I'd think this was one of his schemes to make a name for himself separate from his uncle."

"Hmm, hadn't thought of that. Wonder if he set all this in place before he was arrested?"

"Maybe we should get the sheriff to ask him."

Morgan shrugged again. "Don't think he'll be of much use. We need a real lawman here. Might have to get together with a few other ranchers and hire us a Pinkerton or two to come figure out what's going on."

Royce's thoughts ran in another direction. "I know a guy who is a U.S. Marshall. I could send him a wire if you want. He'd probably come investigate without charging us."

"Let's see what the sheriff says, but it couldn't hurt to wire him. If he comes, great. If not, we aren't out anything. Then we can get together with the other ranchers and talk about hiring Pinkertons."

With a plan in mind now, the two men grew silent. As one, they kicked their mounts into a gallop. They wouldn't know what plan to take until they talked to the sheriff and found out what he was doing about the situation. They would have to do something before whoever was targeting the ranches went too far and killed someone. That thought sobered Royce. He'd have to make sure his men were armed, and start leaving someone at the ranch house until this was resolved.

~

Once in Creede, Royce and Waylon rode straight to the sheriff's office. As they climbed down from their horses in front of the jail, they saw Archibald Grady walking out of the front door. "What is going on?" Royce asked. "How in the world is that man walking free after what he did to all those women?"

Waylon shook his head. "Let's go see, but I get the feeling, we're not going to like the answer."

The two men entered the sheriff's office in front of the jail. Royce wasted no time walking up to the dark-haired man sitting behind the desk like he didn't have a care in the world. "How can I help you gentleman?" His voice was filled with sarcasm, letting them both know they weren't going to be getting any real help from "Black Jack" Ketchem. Royce placed his hands on the desk and leaned toward the sheriff who hadn't sat forward or even moved since they entered the office. He was tired of this puffed-up toad acting like he was better than the men he was supposed to work for. "Why did we see Archie Grady walking out of here a free man?"

Now Jack leaned forward, his pasty face turning red with anger. "It's not any of your business why I let him go but I'll tell you. I investigated the matter and found no evidence that he was involved in the kidnapping and imprisonment of those women. As a matter of fact, I can't find much proof that those women, for the most part, weren't there because they chose to be."

Royce's voice went frosty with his own anger. "I'm married to one of those women, Jack. I can tell you that my wife didn't choose to be locked in a root cellar. She was on her way to California to become a nanny for a respected family when she was waylaid."

Jack nodded. "That's what she said, but I saw no proof of that. I also know that the only person any of them women saw was Dougal. Even Fontaine only saw Dougal. He claimed to have heard a conversation between Archie and Dougal. That's all well and good, but he never saw who was talking. There wasn't enough evidence to take him to trial, let alone convict him." The sheriff leaned back and crossed his arms over his chest like the subject was closed. Royce wanted to smack some sense into the pompous windbag but knew that would just get him arrested.

Waylon cleared his throat. "That wasn't the reason we came to see you, Jack. We want to know what you are going to do about the ranchers who are being harassed and stolen from?"

The sheriff finally stood. "You men sound like a broken phonograph. I done told you I don't have the manpower to go chasing down rumors. My job is to keep the miners and cowboys who come to town in check and to make sure no one actually hurts that silly woman who keeps trying to pick a fight with the men who want to relax in the saloon on paydays. Why the preacher won't keep her up there in Bachelor is beyond me. You want to have people running around looking for rustlers that don't exist, be my guest."

Royce shook his head and looked at Waylon. "Let's go, we're wasting our time. Obviously, if we wanted justice we should have paid for it like Mr. Anders does."

Sheriff Black Jack stepped from behind his desk and stood nose to nose with Royce. "You accusing me of something, Clark?"

Royce shook his head. "Just stating the facts as I see 'em, Sheriff."

"You'd better be careful, boy. It would be a shame for that pretty new bride of yours to become a widow so soon after yer wedding."

Royce's hand dropped to his gun belt. "Is that a threat?"

Black Jack smiled, but it didn't reach his eyes and, contrary to his words, Royce knew it was a threat. "Not at all. Just a gentle warning to be careful, Mr. Clark. The trail back to your ranch is a long, lonely stretch and if you and Mr. Morgan are right, then someone has it in for you ranchers. I'd hate to see you run into the wrong person on your way home. That's all."

Royce's hand itched to take action; every fiber of

his being wanted to draw against the crooked lawman, but all that would do was put him on the end of a rope and leave his family without him. Thankfully, Waylon reached out and slapped him on the back. "Come on, Royce, let me buy you a drink and we'll talk about hunting for those rustlers since the sheriff told us to handle it ourselves."

Royce let his hand drop to his side and stepped back from the sheriff. "Sounds like a great idea."

He and Waylon nodded goodbye to Black Jack and went outside. They took the reins of their mounts and led them back up the street to Otto's livery stable. After turning their mounts over to him, they headed straight for the telegraph office. They knew it was almost time for Arthur Jameson to close for the evening. Hopefully, he'd be willing to send one last message out for them tonight. Royce wanted to get Nathan Ryder here as fast as he could. If the Preacher or one of his deputies couldn't figure out what was going on, they might have no choice but to send for Pinkertons or start hiring gun hands as well as cowboys.

He really didn't want to have to do that because those were rough men, most of them weren't loyal but worked for the man willing to pay the most. It would also put his wife in close proximity to men he wouldn't trust with her best interest. Even if he was unsure of how he should proceed with her, he didn't want her in a worse situation than the one she'd found herself in when she first set foot in Creede. He didn't like the fact that he'd have to let Marta know that Grady was free. Like the rest of the women captured and held by Dougal, she wouldn't be thrilled to know that the man responsible for their imprisonment was free to try again.

He entered the telegraph office to see Arthur look up at their entrance. "Royce, Waylon, I was just about to close up. What can I do for you?"

Royce spoke, figuring he was the one with the connection to the U.S. Marshal. "Couple of things, Arthur. We just came from the jail. You might want to let your wife and her friend Millie know that Black Jack released Archie today. He said there wasn't enough evidence to hold a trial."

Arthur's face looked as shocked as Royce was sure his did when Jack had told him that. "How can that be? I mean, there was a witness."

Waylon shook his head. "According to the sheriff, Fontaine's word wasn't good enough since he didn't actually see Archie. He even insinuated that the women weren't captives but there willingly."

"That's ridiculous. I know for a fact that Mrs. Fontaine was taken against her will."

Royce nodded. "So was Marta."

That caused Jameson to nod. "I heard you'd married her. Congratulations."

"Thanks. She's good with the children." He sighed, then changed the subject. "Look, that's not the only reason we're here. I need to send a telegram to Redemption, New Mexico. The sheriff refuses to help us hunt for the rustlers and some of the smaller ranchers are now being coerced to sell their spreads. Can you send this message before you close up tonight and keep it and any answer quiet for me?"

"What's the message?"

Royce took a piece of paper and a pencil from the operator and quickly wrote.

To: Nathan Ryder U.S. Marshall, Redemption New Mexico

From: Royce Clark, Creede Colorado

Need your help STOP

Rustlers and possible range war. STOP

Local Sheriff refuses to help STOP

Can you assist STOP

End Message

The telegraph operator looked at it and nodded. "I'll send it right away. I didn't realize you knew

Nathan Ryder. How in the world did you meet a famous gunslinger and lawman like that?"

"Bought Blue from him back in '89. He inherited one of the silver mines out past Topaz. He was here checking on something and I mentioned needing a good cattle pony. He had a few extra mounts with him he'd just picked up from some trainer in Sanctuary, Montana. He came out to the ranch and spent a few days. Was a nice fella. Told me if I ever needed him to send word to Redemption."

"Is it true he's a real preacher, too?"

Royce nodded. "Sure is, came west with his Grandfather to be a circuit rider but things didn't work out. Seemed he was a quick hand with a gun and before you know it, he'd earned a reputation and a badge as well as a church in New Mexico. But what would you expect from Nugget Nate Ryder's grandson?"

"You think he'll come?"

Royce shrugged. "Don't know, but I had to try something."

"Maybe he'll investigate this situation with Black Jack and Archie, too."

"Ya never know with Nathan."

The three men shook hands, and the two ranchers headed over to the saloon tent that Anders was using while he had the Nugget rebuilt. Royce would have one drink and head home before dark. He still had that uncomfortable feeling he'd gotten when Black Jack mentioned him getting waylaid on the way home.

~

Marta had put the three younger children down for a nap. She was cleaning up the lunch dishes and putting her bread into the oven to bake, when she jumped at the voice behind her. "You need to bring the two older ones inside right now." The angel was standing behind her wringing her hands in anxiety. Marta felt the truth of the woman's words in the pit of her stomach and went out the kitchen door and called to RJ and Rachel to come in. She didn't have a good excuse to get them inside, but knowing something serious had to be happening for the angel to be so disturbed, she told them to come test the cookies she'd made for dessert that night. The two tore off for the table and she quickly gave them each two cookies and a glass of milk. Marta could see the angel standing just inside the parlor looking out toward the trail that led in from the town. She walked over to the woman. "Who are you?"

The older woman still looked like she had the first time Marta had seen her. Her grey hair was in a simple bun on the top of her head and she wore dark gray widow's reeds over a simple white blouse. "You couldn't say my true name but you may call me Gloria. I've already told you I'm your angel. I was assigned to you and the Clark children just before we met the first time."

"What has you so worried?"

The angel looked at her. "There are some men coming. I don't want them to see the children. I wish I could keep them from seeing you, but none of the ranch men are close enough to meet them when they get here. I need you to do what I tell you even if it doesn't make sense. Tell the children to stay inside for now, please."

Marta nodded. She didn't know why, but she trusted this angel. She'd proven herself to have a reason for everything she had told Marta to do so far. If she hadn't listened, she wouldn't be here now.

"RJ, Rachel, when you are done with your snack, I need you to stay inside until I tell you otherwise. Stay away from the doors and windows if you can and stay quiet. It's important and I can't explain why right now. Will you do that for me?"

Both children looked at her like she'd gone crazy but they nodded at her. "Thank you. Rachel, maybe you can read for a little to your brother until I tell you otherwise. Okay?"

"Yes, Marta."

"Good. Now you two go back into the hall by the bedrooms. Keep your brother and sisters quiet until I come get you, please."

"Are you going to be all right?"

She smiled at Rachel who looked like she was a bit worried. "I'll be fine. I just need you to do this for me. Consider it your next little game." She winked at the girl and smiled. She could see she hadn't completely calmed the girl, but she would pretend she was. She took a primer and led her brother to the hall where the bedrooms were.

Just about that time, Marta heard the sound of horses and a buggy coming up the trail. The angel was at her side. "Get the rifle off the wall right now. I know you don't know how to use it, but they don't know that. I want you to open the door and pull that lever forward and push it back and then point the thing at the man in the buggy. Then ask if you can help them. No matter what, don't stop pointing the rifle at the man in the buggy."

Marta wanted to shake, but she felt an unnatural calm come over her. She did as she'd been told and took the rifle off the pegs it hung on over the fireplace. She walked to the door, opened it, stepped out onto the porch, and pulled and pushed the lever like the angel had told her to. Marta saw four men on horses and one heavyset man wearing a suit in a buggy pulled by two black mares. She pointed the rifle at the man in the buggy. "Can I help you, gentlemen?"

"You could lower that rifle, ma'am; there's no need for it." The voice of the man in the buggy was like cold slime sliding along her backbone.

"I don't think I will, mister. I don't know any of you and you've yet to answer my question."

One of the men was on a horse almost the color of blood. "You want me to take it away from her, boss?"

The man was in all black, had a scar running along the right side of his face from just under his eye to the end of his jaw just clipping the edge of his lips, pulling them into a half smile even when he wasn't smiling. He seemed to have no hair on his head. His hat was pulled low enough she couldn't make out the color of his eyes but his skin was unusually white, almost like fresh cream. "No, Jasper, I don't think that will be necessary."

The man on the horse just stared at her, and for the first time, Marta felt the fingers of fear begin to crawl across her stomach and squeeze her heart. She'd had men ignore her, and on rare occasions leer at her, but the look this Jasper gave her was pure evil. She felt, rather than saw, the angel come up behind her and lay a hand on her shoulder. "Don't fear; just keep looking at the man in the buggy and don't flinch at anything said or done. I won't allow you to come to harm."

"You still haven't answered my question, mister, and if you don't do it soon, I'm gonna think you mean me and my family harm. You might not like it if that happens."

The man looked at her, and at the rifle held so steady in her hands. "Again, there's no need for violence, ma'am. I'm looking for Royce Clark; I was told this was his ranch. Is he around?"

The angel said in her ear. "Tell him the truth."

"No, he went into Creede to see the sheriff."

The man looked at the others. "I see. Why was he going to see the sheriff?"

"He didn't tell me why. Just that he was."

"I see. Well, will you tell him that a Mr. Oliver Thrilway came by to see him? I represent a party interested in purchasing the Circle C. I'm staying at the Miners' Hotel in Creede and would appreciate a few minutes of his time."

She nodded. "I'll let him know, Mr. Thrilway. Now, would you be so kind as to take your men and leave my ranch?"

The man nodded and smiled. Marta realized it wasn't a pleasant smile and she surprised herself by not shaking. The last one to leave was the one on the blood-red horse. He walked his horse closer to her and looked her up and down like she was standing in front of him without a stitch of clothing on. "I reckon I'll be seeing you again, little lady. Yep, sooner than you might think, too." Then he turned his horse and followed after the others. She stood there on the porch holding the rifle tight until the dust of their trail had disappeared. Then she went in and put the rifle back where it belonged and went to tell the children they could go back outside. She went to pull her bread out of the oven before it burned.

Everything was fine and calm until dinnertime when Marta told Royce all about the men visiting the ranch while they ate. Afterwards, he excused himself and headed over to the bunkhouse to talk to Fuzzy and the men.

Marta had the kids all in bed and had cleaned both the table and the dishes and still Royce hadn't come back. Finally, she sighed and took herself to bed. She fell asleep wishing her husband would spend time with her or at least tell her what was going on. She once again wondered if she'd made a mistake marrying this rancher, even if it did give her the family and home she always wanted. Love must not be part of God's plan for her. She wiped a tear and told herself not to dwell on what she couldn't change. Royce needed her even if he didn't want her. That was her last thought as she slipped into sleep.

CHAPTER 7

Arranging things with Fuzzy and the men had taken longer than Royce had expected. He had already decided to leave two men close to the house before he had heard Marta's story about what had happened with the group of strangers. However, a few things she had said filled Royce with concern. The fact that the man in the buggy talked about wanting to buy the ranch lined up with what Waylon Morgan had told him about what some of the other ranchers had faced. If this was that group, the rustling would start soon and maybe even harassment. The thing out of character with the other ranches was the way the man his wife said was named Jasper had acted toward his wife. As much as he didn't want to, if he didn't hear from Nathan soon, he may have no choice but to hire some gun hands to stand watch over his family and the ranch. He'd worked too hard to get where he was to see it taken away by rustlers and swindlers.

All that ran through Royce's head as he stood at the foot of his bed looking at Marta's sleeping form. His mind went to what the angel had said to him about needing to choose. Would he keep clinging to Lucy and the love he'd had that was now past, or would he honor the vows he'd taken the day before: to love, honor, and cherish this woman, forsaking all others?

That's when it hit him, the thing that had been bothering him since just before he made that vow to Marta. To truly honor that vow, not only did he need to allow himself to love Marta, he had to let go of all he was holding on to with Lucy. His new vows contained the same words his vows to Lucy had contained, including the phrase 'forsaking all others.' To truly fulfill his vows to Marta, he would have to not only try to learn to love her, to allow his heart to be open to love again, but he would have to let go of his devotion to Lucy. He would have to forsake her and choose Marta. Just like the angel had told him.

He quickly dressed for bed and slid beneath the covers, trying not to disturb Marta. He turned to look at her sleeping form. Her back was to him and he was once again struck by how pretty she truly was. Her hair and eyes were lighter shades of brown than Lucy's had been. She was taller and curvier, something that he wasn't really upset by because she fit against him perfectly, as she'd proven this morning during their kiss. Her personality and care for his children also made her desirable. If he'd met her instead of Lucy all those years ago, she might have been the one he'd have chosen. In reality, the only reason he had for not allowing himself to get close to her was his commitment to stay faithful to Lucy. He sighed and tried to quiet his mind. He was just going around and around in a circle over this whole issue and nothing was changing. As he lay there watching his new wife sleep, his own slumber overtook him. For the first time since Lucy died, his dreams weren't filled with visions of her and the future they were supposed to have. No, tonight his dreams were filled with a tall, sandy-brown haired woman with eyes like Tennessee sipping whiskey flecked with gold, and lips as warm as good whiskey made a man feel. Tonight, his dreams were filled with Marta. In his sleep, he reached out and pulled his wife close, wrapping his arms around her.

Marta woke to find herself pulled tight against Royce again. His arm was around her waist holding her against his firm body. His leg twined with hers in a way that would have been appalling if they weren't married. It still felt like a slap in the face to Marta; the only time he seemed to not care about getting close to her was when he was asleep. She knew that was just his body's reaction to having a woman in his bed. He probably had held Lucy like this every night; in his sleep, his body remembered and just reacted. He'd certainly never shown her any indication that he willingly wanted to be that close to her.

Marta carefully extracted herself, not wanting to wake him. She didn't know how long he'd been up last night making plans to keep the cattle and ranch safe, but she would take care of what morning chores she could. While she'd been an orphan and city girl all her life, she did at least know how to gather eggs and milk a cow. Those had at one time been part of her chores at the orphanage. She'd slipped into her work dress and apron and carried her boots out of the room with her. She sat at the table and quickly put her boots on and laced them up. She hurried into the kitchen and stoked the fire so the stove would be warm for breakfast. She filled the pot and added the coffee grounds; the coffee would be hot and strong when breakfast was ready. She grabbed the milk bucket and hurried across to the barn. She milked the cow and gathered the eggs. She'd just started mixing up a batch of biscuits when Royce walked into the kitchen. "Marta, we need to talk about a couple of things."

Her heart raced. Had he decided he didn't want to be married to her? Was he going to send her away? Had he decided, like everyone else, he didn't need the orphan no one wanted? "Can we talk while I finish fixing your breakfast? Or should I just go pack my things now?"

Royce's face looked confused. "Why would you go and pack? Don't you want to be here with us?"

Marta spun to look him in the eye. "You weren't going to tell me that I needed to leave?"

Royce shook his head, walked around to where she was, and took her hands in his. "Why would I send you away? We've been married three days today; you've only been on the ranch one full day and part of the day before, and you've already done a great deal to clean up the mess it took me two months to make. I'd be a fool to ask you to leave. No,

I wanted to tell you what was going on and what I expect from you until this mess is cleared up."

"Oh."

He let her go and sighed. "First, you need to know that Sheriff Ketchum let Archie go yesterday."

Marta gasped and stepped back. "What? Why?"

"He claimed there wasn't enough evidence to hold him. That all the evidence they had pointed to Dougal. So if you need to go to town for any reason, I want you to take one of the men with you. Or wait and let me go with you."

"Surely he won't try and grab women off the street again. There would be no doubt who was involved this time."

Royce shook his head. "I don't know what Archie would or wouldn't try, but I do know that Creede isn't a safe town for a woman to walk around alone in. It's getting better, but I'd still like you to be escorted by someone I trust."

Marta frowned and started to tell him she'd been taking care of herself for a long time. Then she thought about what he was saying and could see that he was just trying to protect her. "All right. I'll make sure you or one of the men is with me when I need to go to town."

Royce smiled at her. "Thank you. Now just so

you know, the rustling is only a small part of the trouble ranchers are having right now. I learned last night that someone is trying to buy up ranches, and once they make an offer, all sorts of things start happening around their ranches."

"What kind of things?"

"Hands have been beaten and told if they were smart they'd ride off. Fences have been cut and cattle stolen. Barns and houses have been burned. Typical persuasion tactics a certain type of person uses. So, Fuzzy and I have worked it out so that there will be someone here on the porch at all times. One of the wranglers will also always be in the barn. Their jobs are to watch over the buildings and to keep you and the children safe. I also want you to promise me that if you see any of those men that were here yesterday, you'll let the man out front know and take the children and hide in the root cellar until one of our men comes and gets you."

Marta put the biscuits in the oven while she thought about Jasper's pale face and dark eyes and the way he promised he'd see her again soon, and nodded. "Of course, Royce, if that's what you think is best."

She went to the icebox, got out the bacon, and

sliced several pieces for them. She placed them in the skillet to start cooking and turned back to Royce.

"What would be best is if we could catch these rustlers and convince the men trying to pressure ranchers to sell that we aren't worth the effort it's taking to run us out."

Marta could see that Royce was worried, not just for her and the children but his neighbors and friends, too. She put a hand on top of his and squeezed. "Won't the sheriff do something about all this?"

Royce shook his head. "No, he told us it wasn't his job. I've sent a telegram to someone I know who might be able to help, but I don't know if he'll come, or even if he does if he'll be able to help us."

"We'll just have to pray that he can, and that he will."

Marta's heart skipped a beat when Royce smiled at her. He pulled her into his arms and placed a quick chaste kiss on her lips. "Yes, we will. Thank you for not trying to fight me on this."

She wrapped her arms around his neck. "I wanted to at first, but I realized you are just trying to keep me safe. I've never had anyone care enough about me to do that before. I've always had to look out for myself."

Royce kissed her again. She could tell he was struggling with showing her affection, but he was trying. "Well, now you do have someone who cares, and I'll take care of you as best as I know how."

Marta's whole body warmed at his words. She'd need to be very careful or she'd find herself falling in love with her husband. With that thought still ringing through her head, she extracted herself from his arms. She patted him on the cheek before turning her attention back to fixing breakfast. Yep, she'd have to be very, very careful.

~

For the second day in a row, Royce found himself in Creede. This time he came to check and see if there was a response to his telegram. There wasn't yet, but Arthur Jameson told him that when the answer came, he and Beatrice would come to visit so that no one would suspect Royce was waiting for a telegram. Royce thanked the man who until recently was a man who kept to himself.

Next, he went to both the dry goods and the mercantile and asked the clerks at each to fill the order Marta had given him. He informed them both he'd pick them up later that morning as he had an appointment with a businessman who was staying at the hotel.

Royce walked toward the hotel slowly, looking at the changes in the town. Already frames were going back up for the business that had been burned. He knew he could make a lot of money if he sold the timber on his land right now. He didn't know why he was resisting selling the timber rights to Mr. Anders unless it was because he just didn't trust the man. For some reason, Mr. Anders never seemed satisfied. He already owned several mines, every saloon in Creede, several of the lots that the miners' tents were on, and a few of the homes. Rumor was he owned the Miners' Hotel as well, but no one knew if that was true. The manager refused to talk about the owner and only referred to him or her in passing as "the owner." The town was changing. Even with Archie free again and Black Jack still sheriff, there was a feeling of newness and new beginnings. Only two months ago, people who lived here saw Creede as a place that wasn't fit to raise a family. Now that was starting to change. A large part of that was because of Reverend Bing. His advertisements in eastern newspapers calling for families and business people to move to Bachelor and help make

the town a place for families was slowly changing
not just the face of Bachelor but of Creede, too.
There were more families on the streets. Women
and children were part of the background now, not
hidden inside for fear of being accosted. Oh, Royce
was sure there was still going to be problems and
maybe even some growing pains, but Creede was
changing.

He stopped in front of the Miner's Hotel. The
three-story whitewashed building wasn't anything
fancy, but it was the only hotel in Creede. It was
almost always full as it was the only place a traveler
could stay. There were a couple of boarding houses
but they were more for long-term residents. This
was the place that Mr. Thrilway had told Marta he
was staying. Royce wanted to know what made this
man, or any other for that matter, think they could
just ride onto a man's property and expect him to
sell to them. He also wanted to get a look at the man
Marta had told him had made a personal and very
ungentlemanly threat toward her. Royce would hear
the man out about the offer, but then he'd make it
plain that his ranch wasn't for sale. He'd also make
certain this "Jasper" knew threats or worse against
his family would not be tolerated. Royce might not
be as quick as the Preacher but he wasn't a slouch

when it came to gun work, either. If this Jasper fellow knew what was good for him, he'd heed Royce's warning today.

Royce entered and walked right up to the desk. "I'm looking for a Mr. Thrilway. I was told I could find him here."

The clerk behind the desk nodded and pointed at the dining room to Royce's left. "Mr. Thrilway and company are in the dining room at present."

Royce nodded, "Much obliged."

He turned and entered the dining room. It wasn't hard to figure out which man was Thrilway. He was the only man in a suit and he looked like he weighed at least four hundred pounds. He was as round as a heifer ready to drop a calf. His black hair was slicked back, and his pencil-thin mustache was waxed and curled. His suit was exactly what Royce expected it to be, a black double-breasted with a white shirt and black bow tie. A bowler hat sat on the table at his left hand. He looked like the type of man someone would send to make a slimy offer to buy a man's livelihood for less than it was worth. Sitting to his left was a man whose skin was as white as fresh cream. He was dressed all in black like a gunslinger. He hadn't removed his black Stetson that was pulled low on his head, hiding his eyes in shadow.

While the dandy didn't even look up at Royce's approach, the gunslinger let his fork settle on his plate, and his hand went below the table. Without even looking, Royce knew it was resting on top of his revolver.

Royce walked right up to the table, keeping the gunslinger in front of him. He glanced over at the dandy who was still stuffing forkful after forkful of food into his mouth. "You Thrilway?"

Without pausing in stuffing his mouth, the dandy nodded. "I'm Mr. Thrilway. How can I help you?"

Royce wouldn't look away from the dangerous one. The man was staring just as hard at Royce as Royce was at him. "Name's Clark; my wife said you and several armed men came to my ranch to talk to me yesterday."

The man finally put down his fork and wiped his mouth on his napkin before reaching inside his jacket and pulling out a small notebook. "Clark, Clark…" He ran his fingers down the page before turning to another, stopping about halfway down the third page. "Ah yes, Royce Clark, owner of the Circle C. Sixty-five thousand acres, some timber-land, the rest grazing land. One ranch house, barn, bunkhouse, and foreman's hut. Plus a chicken coop and several line shacks. Estimated a thousand head of cattle." He looked up at Royce. "Have a seat, Mr. Clark. I have a proposition for you."

Royce pulled out the chair facing the quite pale-skinned man, and without taking his eyes from the other man's, slowly seated himself allowing his right hand to rest on the handle of his Colt as well. "I'm listening."

The man cleared his throat. "I represent a party that is interested in purchasing your ranch and cattle from you. The party is willing to pay you two dollars an acre and fifteen dollars a head for the cattle. They will also purchase any of the horses you wish to sell at ten dollars each."

Royce couldn't not look at the slimy toad sitting to his right. "You're joking. I paid more than that ten years ago when I purchased the spread, and there wasn't a single building on it."

"I assure you that this offer isn't a joke. It is what my employer is willing to pay, and I suggest that you consider it very seriously."

Royce shook his head. "Mr. Thrilway, let me make a couple of things very plain to you and your men. First, the Circle C is not for sale. Certainly not at that price, but honestly, not at any price. It's my family's home. We have blood, sweat, and tears in that land, not to mention loved ones buried there.

Secondly, you and your men are not welcome on my ranch. I don't appreciate coming home to a wife who is upset because a man with several heavily armed thugs paid her an unexpected visit. Finally, and this is more for your pet there." Royce pointed at the gunslinger who hadn't said a word the entire time. "If you make any more rude remarks or threats to my wife or any member of my family, I will show you how we treat yellow bellies like you here in Colorado. I hope I've made my position plain to you fellas."

The gunslinger spoke, his voice as cold as the stare he was still giving Royce. "Be careful, cowboy. You have no clue who you're talking to and threatening."

Royce leaned forward so that the gunslinger could see his warning had no effect on him. "You don't know who you're dealing with, either, slick."

The overweight messenger put his notebook back in his pocket. "I would strongly advise you to rethink your position, Mr. Clark. My employer doesn't take well to not getting what he wants."

Royce stood and placed his Stetson back on his head. "That's his problem. I don't take well to threats against me and mine. You can tell your boss the only way he'll get my ranch is over my dead body."

The pale-skinned gunslinger smiled. "That can be arranged."

The fat cat put a hand up. "Mr. White, that isn't necessary."

Royce's eyes narrowed with recognition. "Jasper White, they call you the Ghost?"

The other man nodded. "They do. I see you've heard of me."

Royce nodded. "Yeah, I've heard of you. They say you're a low-life gun for hire who thinks he's a quick hand with a gun. They say you'd shoot your own ma for a dollar."

Jasper laughed. "A dollar! I shot her for free."

Royce shook his head. "I'll only say this to you once more. Stay away from my ranch and family. I won't warn ya again."

"You tell the little woman I'll see her later."

Royce pointed at the man. "Don't test me on this, White."

The gun hand laughed and picked up his fork and started putting food in his mouth as Royce slowly backed out of the dining room. He quickly headed out of the hotel and back to his wagon. He needed to get his supplies loaded and get back to the ranch. This wasn't going to be the end of it. In fact, Royce was pretty sure it was just the beginning.

CHAPTER 8

A week had gone by, and Marta felt like she was mostly settling into her new role as wife and mother. Well, more like housekeeper and governess. The one thing that did not seem to be moving forward at all was the way Royce treated her. She still woke to him holding her close but when they were awake, he seemed to do everything he could to avoid her. She knew he was working later and while he still kissed her, they were more like the one he gave her at their wedding instead of the one he gave her in the kitchen the first time she asked.

Marta realized that she shouldn't have expected that Royce would show her affection when they'd married for no other reason than to make sure his children and home were cared for and to free him up to go back to focusing on working the ranch. That still didn't stop her heart from wanting more. The children treated her like a caretaker more than a mother; she knew it was because they saw how their father treated her. She was a part of their family, but she didn't feel like she was part of it. The only things that were different from when she'd been a nanny was she now was in charge of taking care of the house, her last name had changed, and she didn't sleep alone in a room in the attic.

She sighed as she started working on breakfast for Royce and Fuzzy. They'd both be in soon from their morning work. She knew that they'd come in together. Since that first day when she'd asked Royce to kiss her in the kitchen, he'd made it a point not to come in until Fuzzy was ready to come in. She assumed it was because he didn't want to be alone with her. She knew he didn't love her, but it appeared, he didn't even want her like a husband wanted a wife. She was destined, it seemed, to be in a loveless marriage. She should have found another solution for her problem. Why would that angel encourage her to marry when there was no chance of love in it? If she ever showed her face again, Marta would ask her.

The door opened, and Royce and Fuzzy came in.

Marta sat coffee and cups on the table and went back for the eggs, fried potatoes, biscuits, and sausage gravy. They had all just sat down and Royce had said grace when there was a pounding on the door. Royce went to see who it was; they were shocked when one of the ranch hands who'd been on night patrol was standing there. "Boss, we got problems. The fence has been cut along the southern border and we're missing twenty head of cattle."

Royce frowned, "Did you follow the tracks?"

The young cowboy nodded. "That's the problem, boss. There's horse tracks with the cattle ones. They went into the mountains and we lost them in the rocks."

Royce swore and looked back at Fuzzy. "Rustlers."

The old man nodded. "Yep, guess we know fer a fact it ain't rumors now. Want me to send someone for the sheriff?"

Royce shook his head. "Won't do any good. I'll go see if there's been any word from my telegraph. If not I'll send another one, or I'll go talk to Waylon Morgan about hiring those Pinkerton Agents." Royce looked at the cowboy who brought them the news. "Jake, go get some food and then get some rest. Fuzzy will get a couple of the men to go fix the fence."

Marta spoke up. "Royce, let Jake have some of this breakfast. He deserves it after the night he's had."

Royce nodded. "You heard the little lady, Jake. Come eat with us."

The cowboy took off his hat as he entered. "Thank you, ma'am. I reckon the boys will all be jealous when they find out I got out of having to eat Cookie's hash fer breakfast."

Marta smiled. "Dig in, Jake. Then you do what Royce said and get some rest. I assume we're all going to be busy if the rustlers have finally started working on our herd."

The men all nodded at her words, and Royce sighed. "Now I just have to catch 'em and prove they're working for that Thrilway fella. Wish we could find out who he's working for."

The men nodded, and they all got quiet as they dug into the food on the table. When it was gone, Jake excused himself and headed for the bunkhouse and some well-deserved rest. Marta started clearing the table as Fuzzy and Royce talked about which men they'd send where for the day. When the sound of several horses coming up the trail could be heard, Royce and Fuzzy both stood. Royce grabbed the riffle off the pegs over the fireplace. He turned and looked at Marta. "Go into the back and keep quiet until we find out who this is."

Marta nodded and did as he said. She was worried it was that Jasper White and his men again. He told her he'd be back, and Royce had told her he was a gun for hire known as the Ghost. He had a reputation for shooting men and taking what he wanted. Marta knew from the way he looked at her that what he wanted in Creede was her, and that scared her worse than anything she'd ever felt before.

$$\sim$$

R oyce walked out on the porch with the rifle ready in case the people coming were the rustlers or Thrilway and his escorts again. He smiled as he saw who was riding up to his ranch. Leading about ten men was a man on a black stallion with white mane and tail. His badge was prominently displayed on his black duster. "Well, I guess that answers one question we had, Fuzzy."

The old man was still somewhat cautious. "What's that, boss?"

"If my telegram made it to New Mexico, that is Marshal Nathan Ryder, otherwise known as The Preacher."

Nathan and company pulled up in front of the ranch house. Royce stepped down off the porch to meet him. "Nathan, I'm sure glad to see you."

The marshal swung out of the saddle and walked up to Royce. The two men shook hands. "Royce, sorry I didn't wire you back. I didn't get your telegram until the day before yesterday. I was already headed this way. Felt like I might be needed here soon."

"As usual, your feeling was correct. We got a serious problem going on here."

"Well, I brought my deputy and eight ranch hands with me. You want to tell me why I felt the need to do that?"

"Let's get you and your men settled, and then we can talk."

Nathan nodded. "The boys brought tents if we need them. I would appreciate it if there might be a place my wife and kids can stay; it would save me from having to ride into Creede to stay in my Pullman with them."

Fuzzy spoke up. "You and yer family can have my place, Marshal. I'll bunk in with the hands. Yer men can bunk in with them, too. Well, most of them anyway. We might consider sending a few out to some of the line shacks after we all talk."

Nathan nodded to the foreman. "Much obliged."

Royce smiled. "Nathan, this is my foreman, Fuzzy Knight. As he already offered, I reckon Grace and yer young'uns can stay in his place. I warn you, though, it ain't what they're used to."

Nathan laughed. "You forget, Royce, I run a ranch too. While my place may be bigger, they know what a typical foreman's house is like. Especially an old bachelor one. I'll send one of the men back to bring Grace, Cindy, and the boys out if that's all right. I know Grace was looking forward to catching up with Lucy."

"Umm. Lucy passed away about two and a half months ago."

Nathan put a hand on Royce's shoulder. "I'm sorry, what happened?"

"She passed giving birth to my baby. I ummm… I had no choice but to remarry for the sake of the kids. My new wife is inside." Royce looked at Fuzzy, "Will you go let Marta know it's okay and to expect company. She may need to cook up some more breakfast; I doubt Nathan and his men have eaten yet."

"I'll let her know." Fuzzy disappeared inside to tell Marta what was going on. Royce looked at Nathan. "Let's get your boys settled. Then I'll tell you why me and some of the other ranchers sent for you."

Nathan nodded. "Sounds good. I'll send my deputy back for Grace and have him give her a heads-up about the changes in your family."

Royce cleared his throat. "Thanks, I appreciate it." They walked to where the ranch hands were all dismounting. Nathan gave a few orders, and they watched as the men took the horses to the barn to brush them down before taking their stuff to the bunkhouse. Nathan's deputy dismounted and took his horse over to the trough by the pump to drink some water before he mounted back up to go retrieve Nathan's family.

"Come on in and let me introduce you to my wife Marta. Her story is one you need to hear, too. We might keep you busy for a while, Nathan. There's more than one problem in Creede right now."

"Yeah, I saw that the town had a fire recently."

"Yeah, and that's the least of our problems. Let's go get you some food and coffee and we'll explain. I'll send for the other ranchers later and let them know you're here.

"Sounds good. Let's get started."

Royce led Nathan into the house with lighter steps than he'd taken for the last week.

~

Nathan Ryder stood inside the foreman's cabin on the Circle C ranch. His wife, Grace, and children had just arrived, and he was helping Grace get everything situated for their stay. "I don't know how long we're going to be here, Grace. There're a lot of things I feel like God sent us here to help with."

Grace smiled at him and placed a hand on his cheek. "Nathan love, you know I'm fine with whatever God has planned for us. Is it something you want to talk to me about?"

Nathan nodded. "First, there are some problems in Creede so I'd appreciate it if you wore your gun belt if you go to town. There were some women snatched about six months ago. Royce's new wife was one of them. The man responsible was just released by the sheriff."

"Why would he let a man like that go?"

"He told Royce and another rancher there wasn't enough evidence. However, it sounds to me like he might be on someone's payroll."

Grace shook her head. "Why is it we always seem to be drawn into these situations?"

"Part of our mission, I reckon."

Grace kissed him and then looked around at the messy foreman's cabin. "So obviously, I'm going to need to clean this place up. I'll go meet Royce's new wife and see if I can get some cleaning supplies from her. I'll never understand how you men can live like this."

Nathan laughed. "It just doesn't seem to matter to us as much as it does you. I can send for Stillman to come help you if you want. He's as picky about cleaning as you women are."

"You leave Stillman alone. He needs to stay with the Pullman. You know how much he worries when you pull him from his duties." She bit her lip, "What do you think about the new Mrs. Clark?"

Nathan looked his wife in the eye. "I like her. She seems like a good woman. I can tell you that Royce is struggling. It was obvious from talking to him that he's in love with her. I just don't think he knows it. I get a sense that he might feel guilty since it has only been a couple of months since Lucy passed."

Grace nodded. "Well, I hope he figures it out quickly. I can't imagine what his new wife must be going through; taking on a whole family and a husband who is clinging to his past. That has to be tough."

Nathan hugged his wife. "Maybe that's why you're here, Grace, to be someone she can talk to. All I know is, we're here for a reason. I don't often get a calling that includes taking you, you know. This time I was just as sure you needed to come as I did."

"I know. I'll keep my eyes open for the reason God has us here. On a different subject, why is it every Lucy we know seems to die young?"

"I don't know, darlin'. I hadn't even thought about it."

"We've been married six years and we've lost three in that time. I just find it strange."

Nathan shrugged. "Who knows what God's plan is? Let's see if we can figure out what He brought us to Creede for and then get back home. I'd like to make it by fall round up."

"Yes, and I'm sure your father would appreciate it

if you spent some time in town and fulfilled your part of the Reverendal duties at the church, too."

Nathan laughed. "Probably."

He kissed Grace once more and headed out to meet Fuzzy and Royce. They were going to see if they had any better luck tracking the rustlers than the ranch hands had.

CHAPTER 9

Marta stood in the center of the front room of the foreman's cabin. She'd come with Grace to clean the place. She'd offered when Grace asked for some cleaning supplies and a bucket. It seemed that Fuzzy was as much a slob as Marta's new husband was. "I'm so sorry the place looks like this. If I'd known you were coming with your husband, I'd have cleaned it."

Grace laughed. "Don't worry about it, Marta. This is nothing. You should see what our stable manager's place looks like. I don't think Sandy Bob has ever cleaned that place as long as I've known him. Why, my friend Maryanne and I tried to clean it once and gave up. We figured if it didn't bother Sandy Bob, maybe it shouldn't bother us."

Marta laughed along with the red-haired woman.

"Do you do this often? Travel with your husband when he goes to do marshal assignments?"

Grace shook her head. "No. Honestly, this is only the second time I've ever gone with him when he felt a calling to go somewhere."

Marta's forehead wrinkled. "A calling? What's that?"

Grace stopped and turned to look Marta in the eye. "My husband gets these feelings that he and his family believe are from God. They are never wrong and they always send him somewhere that his special skills are needed. His grandfather, Nugget Nate, used to get them, too. About a week and a half ago, he got one that he needed to bring some ranch hands and come to visit Royce. Only this time he was adamant that I needed to come along. So tell me, Marta, why did God send me to you?"

Marta burst into sobs. Just this morning she had been wishing God would send her a married woman she could talk to, one who might be able to help her understand why an angel told her to marry a man who couldn't, or wouldn't, love her. Now here was Grace Ryder asking her why God would give her husband a message sending her to Marta.

Grace was suddenly wrapping her arms around

her. "My goodness, honey, it was a simple question. I didn't think it would cause that kind of a response."

Once she got her crying under control, Marta pulled back. "You don't understand. I needed someone I could talk to about all this, but I would never have told anyone my whole story until you just told me what you did."

Now it was Grace who looked confused. She pointed to the small table indicating Marta should sit. "Well, I'm here; tell me what I can do."

Marta and Grace sat. "I don't know. I just know I need advice, and I had no one who I thought could understand. You see I never intended to get married."

The whole story poured out of Marta. How she was left on the orphanage doorstep and no one ever seemed to want to adopt her. How she never had a beau or caught the eye of any man. How she had become a nanny and when that position ended, she'd answered an ad for a nanny position in California. She went on to tell about being abducted and thrown in the root cellar. How she and Julianne had finally escaped, and the fight with Dougal that caused his death. Then she told about the letter from the family in California and the strange woman who claimed to be an angel who told her to go to the mercantile and then to marry Royce Clark. When she was done, she sat there watching as Grace thought about the whole thing.

"That sounds like God has a plan for you, Marta. Why would that upset you?"

"Because my husband doesn't want a wife; he wants a housekeeper and nanny. He gave me his name and I thought I was getting my prayers answered with a husband who would come to love me, or at least want me, and a family that would be mine. Instead, my husband doesn't want to be alone with me. He has no desire even to kiss me, let alone the things you hear a husband wants. The children call me by my name and made it plain from the moment I married that I'm not their ma and never will be. I don't understand why even God thinks I don't deserve love. What's wrong with me?" She burst into tears again.

Grace sat there looking at her. "Well, that is a lot. You've been through a lot in the last few weeks, haven't you? Tell me, Marta, how long ago were you thrown in that root cellar by this Dougal fellow?"

"Just over two months ago."

"So before Lucy Clark died."

"I believe so."

"So God used the actions of a couple of evil men

to make sure that you were here on the one day when Royce Clark was so overwhelmed by trying to be a rancher and take care of his family after his wife's death, and you think God isn't a loving God?"

"I didn't say God isn't loving; I said He doesn't think I deserve love. I'm in a marriage and family that don't love me. They may never love me."

Grace shook her head. "That's not true. I've only been here a few hours and I can tell you those kids adore you. Okay, so they don't call you Ma or anything but your name, but they want to be with you. I watched those two boys; they think you are wonderful. They loved the food and the little games you had them play to do their chores. Then there's Rachel; she copies everything you do. I watched her. She wants to be just like you. That's love, my dear. The love of a child for a mother. Look at those two little ones. Why, they cling to you just like mine have clung to me since the day they were born. God didn't put you into a place without love. This is all new for them. Remember they are still mourning their mother's death. Give them time.

"As for Royce, honey, that man is so twitterpated it isn't funny. He may not realize it himself yet, but he has feelings for you. As a matter of fact, I think he does know it. I think what he feels for you makes him feel guilty. His first love is barely gone and already he can't take his eyes off his new wife. A wife he didn't expect to feel anything more than gratitude for."

Marta shook her head. "He doesn't, he won't even kiss me. When I force it he kisses me like he would a child."

Grace smiled. "Marta, that's because he's afraid to kiss you the way he feels. I would wager he thinks he's being disloyal to Lucy by even thinking about wanting you the way he does. I saw him and so did Nathan. When you're in the room, he can't take his eyes off you. Honey, you just need to be patient. That angel didn't get it wrong and God is going to give you that loving family. It's just going to take a bit of time."

"Do you think?"

"I know, Marta. Tell you what, let's talk a bit about how you can turn the heat up on Royce and see if we can't get him to at least act on those feelings he's trying not to have."

"What do you mean?"

Grace smiled at her. "I mean, Mrs. Clark, I'm going to teach you how to seduce your husband. When we're done, that man won't be able to deny his desires."

~

Royce looked around the church in Creede. It had been closed since the last Reverend had angered the miners by always preaching against whiskey and loose women. They'd threatened to hang him right here in the church and he'd up and took the next train out of town. Now the only time it was opened was when they needed a place where a lot of people could meet. He'd sent word and gotten Reverend Bing to come and open it for the ranchers in the community so that they could tell Nathan what was going on. He looked around at the men and woman sitting in the church. Waylon was here, as was his mother. Most of the ranchers had shown up, and they all had the same question; what was Marshal Ryder going to do about the men who were destroying their ranches and stealing their livestock?

Royce stepped to the front of the crowd. He'd left Marta at home with Grace Ryder and the children. However, he knew that another reason several of his neighbors had come was to see his new wife. They could see her at roundup if they came to help or at church Sunday in Bachelor if they were there. Today he wanted to focus on getting Nathan the information he needed and make some plans to start catching the rustlers. "Thank you all for coming out on such short notice. I know we are all having the same issues. Our cattle are getting stolen. Some of you have had men run off and fires set. We all believe we know who is behind it but there isn't any proof.

"Most of you, like me, have asked Black Jack to look into it and were told the same thing. It's not his job. Well, I sent a telegram to a U.S. Marshal, and he's here today to look into it for us. This is Marshal Nathan Ryder. Most of you know about his reputation as The Preacher even if you haven't met him before."

Royce motioned to Nathan who stood and walked up front. "Gentlemen, as I understand it, each of you has been affected by this menace. I came and brought a deputy. I also brought eight men; they can help anyone whose ranch hands either left or are laid up. Just let me know. I'll personally come to each of your ranches to see the damage done. All I ask is if you have cattle rustled, you send someone out to the Circle C to get me. I'd like to be in on as many tracking parties as I can. I promise you I won't stop until we stop these rustlers, and if they are linked to this man trying to buy your ranches, I'll see them all in jail or hung for their crimes."

"What if we don't catch 'em, Marshal? We know you have your own ranch and territory in New Mexico. How long you willing to stay?"

Nathan nodded. "You're right, partner. I can't stay indefinitely; I do have to get back to my own territory and my own ranch. I'll make you this promise. If by the end of August we ain't ended all this, I'll make sure you have a Marshal here who will stay as long as you need him. I don't just mean to catch the rustlers, but to make sure that the law is being upheld in this area. I've already sent a telegram to the U. S. Marshal headquarters asking for a Marshal to be permanently assigned to this area. They've yet to deny me any such request. I aim to see justice brought to the area. You have my word on that."

The sound of boots on the church's steps turned everyone's head. Everyone watched as Jasper White walked through the open doors. "Your word, you say? I got just one question then, Preacher."

Royce watched as Nathan's eyes narrowed. "What's that?"

"Whose justice are you talking about? I mean,

what you think is just probably ain't the same as what I see as just."

"You a citizen of this community?"

"Me? Nah." The gun hand shook his head and smirked. "I work for the man offering to make this rustling problem not these men's problem anymore. Heck, he'll buy every single one of your ranches; you know that. Then you won't have to worry about rustlers or hands that get busted up or leave. You won't have to worry about waking up to find your house or barn on fire or your family dead." The gunslinger held his hands out like he was blessing everyone. "I don't see why you don't all take him up on his offer and let the Marshal go back to his ranch where he belongs."

"What's your name, cowboy?"

Jasper's eyes hardened "I ain't no cow puncher, Preacher. My name is Jasper White, but most people just call me Ghost. I reckon you've heard of me."

Nathan smiled, but it was obvious it didn't reach his eyes. "Yeah, I've heard of you. I heard you're the type of low life who violates women and shoots children for money. The worst kind of low life there is. Least, that's what I've heard."

Jasper laughed. "That's funny. I heard you were a yellow belly who tries to talk his way out of every gun battle. But you're wearing that badge so that can't be true, can it? Only difference between you and me, Preacher, is I own up to my profession while you try to hide what you are behind a badge and a Bible. If you want to own up to what you are, I'll meet you in the street anytime you say."

Nathan walked up to the gunslinger and looked him in the eye from a foot away. "Let me say this where everyone can hear, and you can see the sincerity in my eyes, Ghost. If I find you're involved in any of the rustling or attacks on these good people, you'll wish I'd met you in the street. I'll see ya hung from the tallest tree we can find in this here town."

"I ain't worried, Preacher. I don't think you could find an egg in a hen house." Jasper looked past Nathan to Royce. "Where's the wife, Clark? I wanted to give the bride a kiss."

The man laughed and turned and walked out of the church building calling over his shoulder. "When you men are ready to sell, you let Mr. Thrilway know. He'll be waiting."

It wasn't long after that when the meeting ended and several of the ranchers came up and shook both Nathan and Royce's hands. Finally, most of them were gone and it was just Royce, Waylon and his mother, Reverend Bing, and a young man dressed like an eastern preacher. The young man approached Reverend Bing. "Reverend Bing, I wondered if I could speak to you about getting the key to this house of God."

Callum Bing motioned to the young man. "Eugene, have you met Nathan Ryder? He's a U. S. Marshal and also a Reverend in New Mexico. Nathan, let me introduce Reverend Eugene Theodore. Eugene, are you sure you want to reopen this church? I thought you were going back home."

The young Reverend shook his head. "I've spent the past few weeks walking around this community. There is so much need for a man willing to stand and preach the consequences for the rampant sin of the people of this community. I'm sure I'm supposed to be that man."

Nathan cleared his throat. "Son, my grandfather used to have a saying that you should take into account if you're going to try and become the shepherd of this town."

"What is that, sir?"

"You're apt to catch more flies with honey than vinegar."

Royce almost laughed at the look of confusion on

Reverend Theodore's face. "I don't see how that applies in this situation."

Callum tried to say it a different way. "What Reverend Ryder is trying to tell you, Eugene, is that you'll bring more souls to Christ with compassion instead of condemnation."

The young man shook his head. "You gentlemen have become too complacent with the sin of the people here in the west. They need to be told that what they are doing is sin and that God will punish it."

Royce spoke up, hoping to keep this young hot head from getting himself killed. "Has anyone told you why this church was closed, Reverend Theodore?"

"No, I don't believe they have."

"It was closed because the last few preachers who've tried to preach here did just what you are suggesting. They tore into the sins of the community, mainly the amount of saloons and soiled doves in town. The first one got beat half to death and moved back east. The second one the miners threatened to hang right here in the church. He, too, left town. If you take the same stance they did, you might end up dead."

"Well, I would count it an honor to die in the cause of Christ."

The older ministers looked at each other. Then Callum handed the key over to him. "If I can help you in any way or give you any counsel or advice as you go along, Eugene, don't hesitate to ask. I'll be praying for you."

The younger man nodded once and thanked Reverend Bing before he walked to the back to look at the parsonage attached to the church. Once he was gone, Nathan let out a deep sigh. "That boy's in for a hard lesson, I'm afraid."

"Yes, but sometimes all you can do is let them learn them. Just like a child," Mrs. Morgan stated.

The men just nodded as they all headed for the door. Even though none of them said anything, Royce knew, like himself, they all agreed with Mrs. Morgan.

Nathan Ryder looked at Royce as they were riding back to the Circle C after the meeting with the ranchers. Nathan could tell that Royce was deep in thought and looked conflicted by whatever he was thinking. "God, how can I help my friend? I know you brought me here for more than catching rustlers." As always when Nathan prayed and listened, that still small voice that directed his life whispered in his mind. He rode closer to Royce. "So tell me how you ended up married to Marta."

"Not much to tell, really. You already know she was one of the women snatched from the street by Archie and his pal Dougal. She'd been on her way to California to be a nanny. When she didn't show up, they made other arrangements, leaving her stuck in Creede."

Nathan looked over at Royce. "She couldn't go home to her family?"

Royce shook his head. "She was an orphan, spent her whole life until she turned eighteen in an orphanage. Then she went to work as a nanny. From what I understand, she's never really had anyone she can call family. The way she talked about her work, I don't think she had any friends, either."

"That's rough. Everyone should have someone to care about them."

"Yeah, I agree. Anyway, Lucy had been gone about two months and I was doing my best to take care of things at the ranch and the kids. However, to be honest, Nathan, I wasn't doing well. I knew I wasn't going to make it much longer the way things were. The kids were running around in dirty clothes. I could barely feed them. We were all getting tired of beans and bacon sandwiches. The boys tried to help as much as they could but none of them knew how to care for young'uns, either. I'd come into town to get the formula for Raeann and some more beans, some things for Cookie, and a few loaves of bread. Anyway, I was in the mercantile with Raeann but had left the others in the wagon. I came out with my box of supplies to see this woman holding Randy, who was crying in her arms. I asked what happened and the next thing I know this spitfire of a woman is chewing me up one side and down the other for leaving the children alone in the buggy."

Nathan laughed. He could just see Marta doing that. Royce laughed with him. "She demanded to know where the children's mother was. That set them all a crying and that upset me. I informed her of Lucy's death and then told her if she thought she could do better taking care of the children, she should marry me and prove it. Shocked me to no end when she told me to take her to find the preacher."

Nathan roared with laughter. "I bet it did, at that."

Royce nodded. "She meant it, though, and I knew I needed help. I knew I wasn't going to find a housekeeper who'd be able to watch the young'uns as well. So I took her to Bachelor and talked to Callum and we were married about half an hour later."

Nathan nodded. "Looks like God provided just what you and Marta both needed. Just when you needed it. So what's the problem?"

Royce looked at Nathan, "What do you mean?"

"I mean I've been at your house all day and I've watched you and her. You seem to be attracted to her. And I know she's attracted to you. All those little touches she gives you and that smile when you look at her. The way she watches you when she thinks you're not watching her. However, I noticed you don't seem to show her any affection. I mean, we left and I kissed my wife and you kissed yours on the forehead like she was Rachel and not your wife."

"I didn't marry her for love, Nathan. I married her for the children's sake."

"Yet you love her."

Royce shook his head. "No! She's attractive. But I don't love her. I love Lucy."

Nathan pulled up on his reins, stopping Storm

and forcing Royce to stop, too. "Royce, are you telling me that you won't show Marta affection because of Lucy?"

"Of course that's what I'm telling you. I made vows to Lucy when we married. You know, to love her, to forsake all others. I'm keeping those vows."

Nathan shook his head. "I'm a preacher, Royce. I know those vows you took. They say until death parts you. Lucy is dead. Your vows are ended."

"No, I aim to keep 'em until death. Just like I promised."

Nathan shook his head. "You know that isn't going to work. You do know that, don't you?"

"What do you mean?"

"I mean that either Marta will come to resent you not loving her the way you vowed you would before God and your house will be filled with bitterness and anger, or she'll leave, and have every right to, since you won't honor your vows to her. But the worst thing that can happen is this. Eventually, your desires and physical needs will overwhelm you. Then you'll exercise your rights, only Marta won't feel loved and cherished; she'll feel used. Instead of the act being one of shared love and passion, it will become a duty she performs. You'll come to resent that she isn't like what you had with Lucy. Eventually, what should have been an example of love will become an expression of guilt and shame. Your guilt and her shame."

Royce glared at Nathan. "You don't get it. I already feel guilty. Every morning when I wake up with Marta pulled up tight against me, my hands in intimate places, I feel like I've cheated on Lucy. When Marta wants me to kiss and spark with her so she becomes comfortable with the physical side of marriage, I feel guilty. Those kisses should belong to Lucy. My response to those kisses should be for Lucy."

Nathan shook his head and walked Storm sideways until he could lay a hand on Royce's shoulder. "But you aren't cheating on Lucy, because Lucy is beyond the need for your love and devotion. Let's look at this another way. What if it had been you who'd died? Would you expect Lucy to be faithful to you the rest of her days?"

"What do you mean?"

"If you'd died, would you want Lucy to remain single and alone the rest of her life?"

"No, of course not. But that's different."

"How is it different? Do you think she wants you to be alone the rest of yours? Don't you think she wanted what you would want for her? She wants you to be happy, to experience love. But to do that you have to let go of vows that are finished. Death has parted you from them, my friend."

Royce swallowed and fought to keep control of his sorrow. "But if I love Marta, then I'm admitting that I don't love Lucy anymore. I can't do that."

Nathan nudged Storm into a walk and Royce followed alongside him. "So you can only love one person at a time?"

"Yes."

Nathan shook his head. "Then I feel sorry for Rachel, RJ, Randy, Rose, and Raeann. It's a shame you have no love to give them."

Royce shook his head. "That's different, Nathan, and you know it. I love them. They're my children."

Nathan looked at him in mock shock. "You mean you can love more than one person at a time? So if that's true, why can't you love Marta without discarding the love you felt for Lucy? Do you think Marta expects you to forget Lucy?"

"No, of course not. She's made it a point to remind the children of their mother. She even told them she wants them to love their mother still. She wants them to know Lucy loved them."

"Then Royce, the only problem I see here is you. You seem to need to punish yourself and you're saying it's out of love for Lucy, but I think it's because you feel you let Lucy down. You didn't; you loved her. You cared for her and now God has given you another wife to do the same for. The question is, are you going to obey His word and love your wife?"

Nathan could see that his questions had hit their mark, so he kicked Storm into a trot. "Let's get back to the ranch. I reckon our wives have cooked up a feast by now."

Together the two men set their mounts to galloping toward the Circle C and a hearty meal.

CHAPTER 10

Marta was prepared to do the things that Grace Ryder had told her would drive Royce crazy. However, all it took was one look at his face when he came in the house to know tonight was not the night to start trying to entice her husband. She didn't know what had gone on, but he didn't look like he was happy. She walked up to him and placed a hand on his cheek. "Royce, is everything all right?"

He looked at her for a long minute before he placed his hand over hers. "We need to talk. Can you see if Grace will keep an eye on Rose and Raeann?"

She looked into his eyes. Had Grace been wrong? She'd told Marta that she was certain Royce loved her, but he just hadn't realized it yet. What if she was wrong and he was going to send her away? After all, no one ever wanted her. Why would Royce be any different? "I'll go ask her."

"Thank you."

She turned and walked into the kitchen where Grace was putting a pan of cornbread on the table to cool while the chili finished cooking. Grace looked at the tears Marta was holding back and pulled her into strong arms. "What is it, Marta?"

"Royce asked me to see if you could watch the little ones. He wants to go talk. I think he's going to tell me he doesn't want me here anymore."

Grace pulled away from her. "Oh honey, don't think like that. You're his wife. He isn't going to send you away."

Marta shook her head. "But I'm not, not really. I'm just the housekeeper and nanny he gave his name to so he wouldn't ruin my reputation. I shouldn't have pushed him to kiss me. He told me he'd never love me. I just hoped I could be enough that he'd want me even if only a little. Will you watch the children, please? The sooner I get this over with the better."

Grace shook her head. "I'll keep an eye on the children, but I think you're wrong, Marta. I'll be praying. Go on now."

Marta nodded and wiped at her face. She took

off her apron, hung it on a hook, and then smoothed her skirt. She walked back to Royce as he stood by the door. He opened it and she went through. Closing the door, Royce took her hand and placed it on his arm. They walked silently side-by-side. Royce seemed lost in his thoughts; Marta was worried about what he was going to say when he finally got everything sorted in his mind. "Was there a good turn out to meet with Marshal Ryder?" Marta finally asked just to break the silence.

"Hmm? Oh yes, most of the ranchers came and those that didn't sent a hand or their foreman. We even had a visit from that Jasper White fella."

Marta gasped at that. "Why would he show up?"

"Mainly to threaten everyone and try to prod Nathan into a shootout. He was careful not to say anything that was criminal but everyone knew what he was saying. But Nathan and his men will find the rustlers and the proof we need to end White's threats. Don't worry about that."

"What did you need to talk to me about?"

"I've been thinking about our marriage."

"Oh?"

Royce nodded. "I don't think I've done right by you. I asked you to marry me out of anger and frustration. I just didn't know what else to do, I was a failure at caring for my children and you seemed like the easy solution. However, you deserve better. You deserve to be married to someone who recognizes you for the amazing woman you are."

"I'm not that amazing."

Royce stopped and looked at her with shock evident in his eyes. "But you are, Marta. I think you might be one of the most amazing women I've ever met in my life. You married me knowing I was only doing it to get help with my house and children. But you've loved my children like they were your own. You've taken care of my house, and you haven't complained once at the way I've treated you. You deserve a husband who will cherish you as the precious gift that you are, not a bitter heartbroken rancher. I want you to know I recognize how special you are."

Then he did something that Marta thought he'd never willingly do; he pulled her into his arms and lowered his lips to hers. His kiss started gentle and sweet, but when she wrapped her arms around his neck, he pulled her tighter against him, his kiss becoming more passionate by the second. When she thought her legs wouldn't hold her up one second more, he gentled the kiss again and finally released her mouth, but not her body. He sighed and it was a sound full of longing and regret. "Be patient with me, Marta. I'm trying to put the past behind me."

She looked up into Royce's blue eyes. "I'm not asking you to put Lucy behind you. Royce. I know you love her still. She's the mother of your children and the woman you thought you'd spend the rest of your life with. I know she will always have part of your heart. I'm just asking if you can find a way to give me a part of it, too."

Royce stroked his hand down her cheek; Marta reached up and caught his hand, turned her head and placed a kiss on his palm. He turned and put his arm around her waist; she rested her head on his shoulder as they walked. Neither felt the need to speak. They just enjoyed each other's presence as they walked. As they topped a ridge, they saw a large oak tree beside a fenced area with a single carved headstone. Royce led her up to the grave. "This is where I laid her. I come up here on occasion and talk to her. I know she isn't really there, but I feel closer to her when I come here."

Marta looked up at him. "Do you want me to go and leave you alone with her?"

Royce shook his head. "No, I brought you up here so I could do what I need to do. I want to introduce you to her and then say something to her."

"Okay."

Royce led them right up to the headstone. He released his hold on Marta's waist and took her hand as he knelt down by the tomb. "Hey Lucy. This is Marta, the woman I was telling you about the other day. She's taking good care of your babies. She even makes sure they hear stories about you and shares their memories of you. She's taking good care of us; I don't want you to worry about that." Tears ran down Marta's face as he stroked Lucy's name just like he'd done her cheek just a few minutes ago. "I love you, Lucy. I always will; but I've come to say good-bye. This will be my last visit. I'm married to Marta now. You know that but I had to tell you again. I'm letting you go, and I'm going to let my heart move on to Marta now. She deserves my love as much as you do. So, good-bye, my love. I'll see you when I get to the kingdom someday." He stood and started to lead Marta away, but she hesitated. "Can you give me a minute with her?"

Royce looked at Marta with something like surprise on his face. Then he nodded and walked away to stand outside the fence. Marta knelt down and laid her hand on Lucy's name. "I promise, Lucy. I'll love your family just like you did. Thank you for letting me be part of the family. I'll love him just as much as you did. You rest in the arms of Jesus. I'll take care of our family." She patted the stone and stood. She walked over to Royce, and he wrapped his arm around her again. She sighed as her head went back to his shoulder. They walked back toward the house with several stops along the way for even more romantic kisses.

When they walked through the door to the house, Marta saw the look Grace gave her and the smile that she couldn't contain. Marta's face burned, knowing that the older woman could tell she had been well kissed. Grace winked and then motioned for them to take a seat at the table. She leaned close to Marta and whispered. "Doesn't look like I need to teach you anything, honey." Marta kept her head lowered to hide the blush that she couldn't control.

≈

Royce couldn't take his eyes off of Marta. Now that he had allowed himself to admit that he was attracted to her, he couldn't seem to think of anything except finding time to be alone with her. Nighttime became the most frustrating for him. He was still taking it slow to let Marta get used to the physical aspect of marriage. But when she snuggled up against him to be kissed and held, he didn't want to take it slow. No, what he wanted was to make Marta his wife in every sense of the word. Yet he knew she needed time to get used to the thought of anything more intimate. He'd go slow and fall more deeply in love with his wife every day.

They'd had a week of peace after the meeting with the other ranchers, but during the second week the rustling and attacks on other ranchers had increased. Nathan and his men were spread over several ranches, following trails and trying to get a line on where the rustlers disappeared. Royce and his hands were busy moving their herd in closer by utilizing the winter grazing fields. This would make it more difficult when the snows came because the fields would have already been grazed. As much as Royce disliked the idea, he was going to have to buy extra hay for the winter and pray that his herd didn't suffer too many losses.

It was Saturday night and he'd promised Marta that they'd go to church the next day. She didn't push him often, knowing that the two hours to Bachelor weren't something they could do every week. But he had always tried to go once a month and he'd told Marta they'd go this week. They could probably go more often now that Reverend Theodore was opening the church in Creede again. He'd informed everyone that the doors would be open the next Sunday. Royce thought he might better go just to make sure the young zealot didn't get strung-up on his first Sunday.

He watched as Marta showed Rachel how to heat the iron on the stove to press everyone's Sunday clothes. He had to agree with Grace Ryder; his daughter seemed to have blossomed under Marta's care. With Lucy, she had been well behaved and helpful; with Marta, she seemed to come alive under the fun games and tricks Marta used to teach the children to help with the chores around the house. At first, he'd been a bit leery of her getting RJ and Randy to help with dishes, laundry, and even mending. RJ was also learning how to help with cooking, just like Rachel. While he wasn't sure about the boys learning how to do women's work, he had to admit that Marta had a point. She'd told him if he'd learned how to cook and do some basic cleaning and mending, then he wouldn't have been so overwhelmed when Lucy had passed.

Marta had pointed out that the cowboy cook was a man and that the cowboys all needed to be able to mend their own shirts and socks. It wasn't something that Royce had ever thought of. He'd worked for his parents until he got married to Lucy, and then they had moved and she'd done all that for him. He was happy Marta also encouraged the boys to spend time helping in the care of both the stable and the horses. She wasn't Lucy, she was different in many ways, but she was exactly what he and his children needed. She was even trying to encourage Rose to walk more and to speak.

She caught him watching her, and her face blushed red. He loved that her face was so responsive. He wondered if she knew how lovely he found her. He'd wait until she sent Rachel to get something and then he'd tell her. He was so blessed. God had given him a second gift of love, one that was exactly what he and his children needed. A woman who longed for a family and a home and completed theirs.

Just as he got ready to tell her to send the children to bed and spend time alone with her, there came the sound of hooves and the shout of men looking for him and Nathan. He watched as she smiled at him and nodded. He grabbed his gun belt and Stetson on the way out the door, then came back quickly and kissed Marta. "I'll be back when I can."

She smiled at him. "I know; go find these rustlers so we can move on with life."

He nodded and slipped out the door. Another night he'd not get to hold his wife as they drifted to sleep. It seemed that since he'd decided to let his heart love her, everything that could get between them, had. Now rustlers again. They had to figure out where they were hiding and put an end to this before someone gave up and sold out to Thrilway, or Jasper White pushed too hard and someone's family was hurt.

CHAPTER 11

For two weeks, Marta had been watching for the return of Royce. He and Nathan had returned early Sunday morning and immediately grabbed gear for an extended search through the high country. They'd followed the tracks of the cattle and rustlers up the mountain until the grass and trees became scarce and the rocks made tracking more difficult. The two men had decided that the only way to figure out where the rustlers were taking the cattle was to search the whole peak and surrounding areas; they were getting supplies and gear for an extended stay in the High Lonesome. Royce agreed with Nathan that the rustlers must have found a hidden valley to graze the cattle because they weren't taking enough at any one time to be running them to a buyer. While Marta hated the thought of Royce being gone for so long, she knew that if they could catch these rustlers, life at the ranch would return to normal. She knew Nathan was anxious to find the rustlers and missing cattle before he had to head back to his own ranch in New Mexico.

She missed her husband. They had finally broken through the walls that were separating them. She had been sure that Royce would make her his wife in every way if they hadn't been split by the needs of the ranching community in Creede. While part of her once again felt like she wasn't an important part of someone's life, she did admire that her husband took his responsibilities to his neighbors as seriously as scripture told him to. There was no denying that Royce Clark loved his neighbors as he loved himself. Now if he'd just get home and love his wife the same way, she'd be thrilled.

She heard the sound of horses coming up the trail. If it wasn't Royce and Nathan returning, then it was trouble. She quickly dressed and grabbed the rifle from its pegs. Unlike the first time she'd taken the gun in hand, she now knew how to use it. Grace Ryder had taken it upon herself to teach Marta the things she thought every woman in the west should know. Marta could now load and shoot the rifle, a shotgun, and even a small revolver. Grace had gifted her with a set of throwing knives, had taught her how to use them, and where to hide them on her person so she was always prepared to defend herself. She still remembered when Grace had told her, "Next time someone tries to grab you and shove you in a root cellar, you'll be ready for them."

She stepped out on the porch and leaned the rifle against the wall as she saw her husband and Marshal Ryder dismount in front of the ranch house. They had six men tied to horses between them. Marta raced down the stairs and threw herself into Royce's arms. "Well now," her husband laughed as he caught her, "What a nice way to be welcomed home."

She smiled up at him and wrapped her arms around him. "I'm glad you're home. We've missed you."

Royce looked down into her eyes and smiled. "I missed you, too, but we got them. Not all of them, but we got these who were watching over the herd. Nathan's men are driving them to the back fields. I'll ride out to the other ranches later today and tell them to pick up their cattle. I don't think anyone will have lost any significant numbers once they claim their beeves."

"So it's over?"

Royce shook his head. "It's not over, but Nathan figures that there won't be any rustling for a while. Especially since we know where they were keeping the cattle. He's going to go kiss his wife and get Deputy Wheeler and they'll take these rustlers over to Topaz. Apparently, Nathan doesn't think it would be wise to put them in the Creede jail. He plans to leave Wheeler here in Topaz to keep an eye on things when he heads back to Redemption." Royce watched as Deputy Wheeler came out of the bunkhouse and walked over to the outlaws still tied to their horses. "I've got them, Mr. Clark. Nathan said for you to go see your family. We'll take it from here."

Royce wrapped his arm around Marta. "So what kind of tasty treat are you going to make me for breakfast? I'm tired of eating Nathan's mountain man food. I swear his Grandpa taught him how to cook every critter in the woods."

They walked in the house and Royce kicked the front door closed. He pulled Marta into his arms and his lips claimed hers. She sighed and wrapped her arms around him, giving as good as she got. When she thought she was going to pass out from lack of air, Royce pulled back and stared into her eyes.

"That's a good start. I've missed your sweet kisses, Marta honey."

She smiled and laid her head against his chest, breathing in the smell of campfires and horse, and under it, all her husband's own unique scent. "I've missed you, too."

He kissed her again and then she pulled away. "Sit down. I'll have some bacon and French toast in just a little bit. The children will be up soon, too. I know they'll be excited to see you as well."

She practically skipped into the kitchen her heart was so light. She pulled on her apron and got to work. She wasn't really surprised when she turned to put the plater of bacon on the work table to see Royce leaning against the door frame watching her. The look in his eyes said more than any words, and she felt her face beginning to warm with another blush. She sauntered over to him, rose up and placed a quick kiss on his lips. "Stop standing there staring at me. Make yourself useful and go wake the children. I'll have food ready by the time you get them to the table."

When she turned her back on him, he grabbed her, pulled her back around, and kissed her soundly. "That should hold me until later. Now I'll see about the young'uns."

She smiled as she thought about what later might entail. Would tonight be the night he finally made her his wife in every way? She hoped so and felt her face heat again at her own thoughts. Then she smiled as she heard Rachel's cry of, "Pa! You're back," followed by the sound of happy children welcoming their father home. She carried the food out to her family. The smiles on their faces were mirrored on her own as she took in the sight of the six people she loved the most in the world. Her family.

~

Royce and Marta watched as Nathan, Grace, and their children waved to them from the back of their private Pullman car. He hated to see them leave. Grace and Marta had become good friends, and Nathan was a great lawman. Still, he understood their need and desire to go home. He thanked God for sending them. Even more than that weird angel, Nathan had helped him see that he was hurting Marta as much as himself by holding on to the vows he'd made to Lucy. He also was grateful to Nathan for helping them catch some of the rustlers and for arranging for the newly promoted Marshal Wheeler to become the official

U.S. Marshal for their area. Topaz had a jail but no lawman; it was the perfect place for Wheeler to operate. The six rustlers they caught insisted that they had worked alone, but Nathan, Wheeler, and Royce all suspected that they'd worked for Thrilway with Jasper White giving the orders.

The question that Nathan told Wheeler to work on answering was who Thrilway and Jasper worked for. Someone was directing the attempted buy out of all the ranches in the area. Royce was glad that wasn't his job to figure out. He figured he'd leave the work of justice to the lawmen. He had cattle to round up in another week and decide how many to drive to Denver. But until then, he had other plans. He was going to woo his new wife and let her know once and for all how much he loved her. That's what he'd come to realize while looking for rustlers with Nathan up in the Tall Pines. He loved Marta. Not he was learning to love her, but that he already loved her with as fierce a love as he'd loved Lucy. Tonight he planned on showing that love.

As the train carrying the Ryders pulled away, Royce wrapped his arm around Marta and led her and their children back to the wagon. He helped them all up into the wagon and only paused for a moment as he saw Jasper White watching them from in front of the Golden Nugget tent. The gun hand just stared at Marta and it angered Royce. He wanted to walk over and knock the man on his rear. Instead, he climbed up beside Marta and pulled her close against him. Then snapped the reins sending the team toward home.

CHAPTER 12

M arta was content. When they'd gotten
home from seeing the Ryders off in
Creede, Royce suggested that they take the children
for a picnic in the back yard. She had quickly gathered some leftover fried chicken, made a potato
salad, and sliced fresh fruit and vegetables. She
poured lemonade into several jars and sealed them.
The food, along with plates, forks, and bread went
into a basket. She grabbed a quilt that they could
spread on the ground and met her family on the
back porch. She and Royce walked with the three
older children between them, all of them holding
hands, making a chain from her to Royce. Marta
carried Raeann and Royce had Rose. They walked
down to the spring that ran through the west side of

the ranch. When they found the perfect spot, Marta let RJ, Randy, and Rachel spread out the quilt. Marta laid a very sleepy Raeann on the edge of the quilt and started to lay out the food. Royce took the other four children down to the spring and let them cool their feet from the early August heat. Once the food was laid out, she called Royce and the children to sit and eat.

They ate, talked, and laughed. Marta had never felt more a part of a family than she did today. Without any of them having said anything, she knew she was loved by each one of them. She looked over at Royce and caught him staring at her like she was the most beautiful thing he'd ever laid eyes on. She felt her face heat with a blush. Royce leaned close, took her face in his hands, slowly pulled her near, and kissed her. The boys made yuck noises, and Rachel giggled. Royce let her go and leaned right up to her ear. "Tonight, Marta. Tonight I'm going to make you my wife in every way." Marta's heart raced as she looked into his eyes. The passion she saw there sent tingles racing through her. She was finally the one someone wanted. No longer was she the one no one wanted; this wonderful man made it plain in words and looks that he wanted her.

Before she could fully recover from that revelation, little Rose climbed up on her lap and imitated her father by placing her cubby little hands on each side of Marta's face and leaned forward to give her a slobbery toddler kiss. "Lub you, mama."

Marta gasped and looked over at Royce. "I'm so sorry. I don't know where she heard that. I've never told her to call me that."

Rachel giggled. "I taught her to call you that."

Marta and Royce looked at the girl. "What?"

"Back when you first came, you said we needed to find a name to call you. The boys and I talked. You might not be our ma, but you're our second ma. So we agreed we'd call you mama; two ma's."

Marta's hands flew to her mouth as she stifled a sob. But she couldn't stop the tears that raced down her cheeks. Royce leaned forward and pulled her into his arms. Rachel looked at them, her face stricken. "Did we do something wrong?"

Royce smiled at her. "No baby. You did something very right. I think that's a good thing for you and your brothers and sisters to call Marta. From now on, we'll all call her mama. Okay?"

They all nodded, but Rachel wasn't convinced. "Why is she crying then?"

Marta reached out and pulled the girl into her

arms. "These are happy tears, Rachel. You've made me very happy. This tells me you want me to be part of your family and that makes me very, very happy."

The little girl hugged her and then ran off to play in the water with her brothers. Marta stood and wiped her face once more. "I forgot a bottle for Raeann; she'll be waking soon. I'll go get it and a fresh diaper. I'll be right back."

Marta walked back to the house thanking God all along the way. How her life had changed. Three months ago, she'd gotten off a train to get some food and had been abducted. Now she was a wife and mother, two things she never thought she would ever be. She had a family that loved and accepted her and a home that was hers. All her fondest dreams had come true but one. She figured if Royce's looks were any indication it was just a matter of time until the last one came true as well. She couldn't wait to feel his child growing in her belly. She walked into the kitchen and had just mixed the formula and put it in the pot of hot water to warm when she was grabbed from behind. "Hello, Mrs. Clark. I told you I'd see you soon."

She caught a glimpse of Jasper White before her vision went black and she slipped into the darkness.

∽

Royce watched as Marta walked away. He was so blessed to have this amazing woman as his wife. He was trying very hard not to get up and follow her back to the house and take her to their room right now. Only the thought of his children left alone near the stream stayed his feet. Instead, he got up and went to play in the water with them.

"The time has come, Royce Clark."

Royce turned to see Daniel standing behind him. "What do you mean? I already made my choice; I let Lucy go and chose to love Marta."

"That wasn't the choice you had to make. Even now evil has come to your house to snatch your new wife away. What will you give to save her? Will you choose her over everything you've worked for?"

Royce stalked up to the angel. "What evil? What are you talking about?"

"The men who want your ranch have sent their servant to take your wife. They will give her back if you give them your ranch. Which will you choose?"

Royce looked back at his children. "Rachel, get your brothers and sisters and come to the house. Mama's in trouble."

With that, he turned and ran as fast as he could for the back door of his home. He yanked it open to hear a sound come from the front parlor. He raced through the house calling Marta's name. He reached the front door to see Jasper White, his arm around Marta, pulling her as she struggled toward his horse. "Hello, Clark. Your bride and I are going for a ride. If you want her back, I suggest you go see Thrilway and sign that bill of sale." The gun hand smiled and nuzzled Marta's neck. "Until then I'll entertain your sweet bride."

He laughed and turned Marta to force his mouth against hers. Royce watched as Marta's right arm moved back and then plunged forward into Jasper's stomach. "You stupid chit; you stabbed me!" the outlaw screamed. He took the hand holding his revolver and slammed it up against Marta's face, sending her flying back into the hitching post in front of the house. The side of her head slammed into the post before she fell in a heap on the ground. Royce raced to her as Jasper collapsed on the ground right in front of his horse.

Royce sat on the ground beside Marta and pulled her into his lap. She wasn't moving. Was she still alive? He couldn't stand the thought of losing another wife. He saw movement out of the corner of his eye and saw Daniel and a woman in gray standing on his porch. The person who caught his attention the most was the dark angel he'd seen once before, the night Lucy passed. Death was here. Royce carefully laid Marta back on the ground. Then he stood facing death with Marta behind him. "You can't have her. I won't allow it."

Death walked toward him. "You can't stop me, Royce Clark. I am Death; I go where I am sent. When I arrive, a soul must be collected."

Royce stood his ground. "Not her. You can't have her. If you must have a soul, then take mine."

Daniel looked at him. "You would choose to die in her place?"

Royce nodded without a second thought. "Absolutely."

The woman beside Daniel spoke in a quiet but firm voice. "No greater love has a man than to lay down his life for another."

Daniel and Death both nodded silently. Then Daniel smiled. "You chose well, Royce Clark. Well done." Then he and the woman were gone. Death stepped around him and whistled. A pale horse appeared and Death, dressed in black like a cowboy, climbed into the saddle. He pulled a lasso of fire from the saddle horn and punched a loop in the end. He set the horse galloping and dropped the loop over Jasper. Royce watched as the lasso caught on the shadow that was the gun hand's soul and ripped it from the blood-soaked body sitting on the ground. Death rode on, dragging the screaming soul of the Ghost behind. Then silence.

Royce sat beside Marta as she moaned and opened her eyes. "What happened?"

"Jasper came to snatch you and force me to sell. But you stuck a knife in his gut. Where did you get that?"

Marta smiled. "Grace thought I needed to be equipped like a western rancher's wife." She reached into her right sleeve with her left hand and pulled out another knife. "I got one in each boot, too."

Royce laughed. "Remind me not to anger you."

Marta smiled, then winced and put her hand to her head. Royce slowly stood and pulled her into his arms, carrying her gently into the house where the children had just entered. "Is Mama all right, Pa?"

"She's fine, but she needs to rest. Rachel, will you feed your sister for me? I need to hitch up the wagon and go see the sheriff."

Fuzzy walked through the front door. "No need,

boss. I'll take care of it. What should I tell Black Jack?"

"Tell him he better do something about that Mr. Thrilway, or I'll get Marshal Wheeler to do it."

"Got it, boss. You take care of the missus and let me handle the trash."

Royce nodded and carried Marta to the bedroom.

~

Much later that night, Marta lay in Royce's arms. He'd kept his word and now she was his wife in every sense of the word. As they lay together, kissing and marveling at the gift of the other that God had given them, Royce took her face in his hand and gently kissed her. "Thank you, Marta Clark."

She frowned. "For what?"

"That day on the boardwalk outside the mercantile, I was sinking. I wouldn't have made it another week. You rescued me. Not just by taking over my house and caring for my children but by opening my heart again to love."

Marta smiled and kissed her husband. "I can't take any of the credit, you know. All of that has to go to that silly angel who told me to go buy lemon drops and accept any proposal that came my way."

Royce laughed. "Maybe so, but you chose to do what she said. So you still rescued me."

Then he pulled her close and showed her again just how thankful he was. Later, after he was sleeping, Marta slipped out of bed and slipped on her nightgown. She picked up Raeann and slipped out of the room. She knew the baby would wake about the time she had a bottle fixed. She walked into the kitchen and wasn't really surprised to see Gloria sitting at the worktable. "Do you still wish I'd left you alone, Marta Clark?"

"No, Gloria, I admit you were right."

"Well, not me, but the BOSS. You know you were wrong all these years, don't you?"

Marta shook her head. "What do you mean?"

"You've always thought no one loved you or wanted you. The BOSS loved you. He always wanted you. You are precious, not just to this family, Marta, but to HIM. Never forget that."

The angel stood and walked to the kitchen door.

"Will I ever see you again?" Marta asked.

The old woman stopped and looked back and smiled. "I doubt it, but I'll be around. Your four daughters are also my responsibility." Then she walked through the door. "Four? But…."

Marta smiled as the meaning of what the heavenly guardian had said hit her. All because she thought she was rescuing the rancher.

George McVey always wanted to be a superhero; sadly, no radioactive storms or animals have been a part of his life. One day while spinning a tall tale for his family, some suggested once again that with all his experiences in ministry, and his imagination, he should be writing books. This time it was like lightning struck him and he decided, *why not?*

Since then George has been hard at work using his creative imagination and writing several books. He's still adding to his bibliography to this day.

George lives in the wonderful state of Almost Heaven, West Virginia. A few years ago, he moved from a single-family home to a deluxe apartment in the sky, well the fourth floor anyway. He lives with his wife of thirty years and a service dog named Daisy Mae. He is visited often by his three children and two grandsons.

If you ever come to visit him, you will probably find him sitting in his lazy boy recliner or at his desk in the corner office working on some writing project. If it's not a teaching book, then it's a novel. If he isn't working on a novel, then he will be working either on a short story or blog post. If he isn't doing either of those then he is either asleep or eating, his other two favorite past times.

You can reach him by email at pastor.george.mcvey@gmail.com. You can also find out more about his books, get a free book, or join his beta readers team to help make the books he writes better at his website georgemcvey.weebly.com. You can also connect with George on Facebook at his author page https://www.facebook.com/George-H-Mcvey-557196424346233.

If you would like to read good clean books, then you might find any or all these Facebook Readers Groups helpful. You can meet authors and talk with them and other readers about their books there. Christian Indie Authors and Readers group, Sweet Wild West Readers Group, and Pioneer Hearts Readers groups. George is part of all three.

Join the Silverpines's Readers Group on Facebook to stay caught up on all the Silverpines's action and talk with other fans of the series and authors.

∽

WHAT'S NEXT FOR COWBOYS AND
ANGELS

Have a blast hanging out in Creede, Colorado?
There's more where that came from. Visit
www.sarajolene.com/cowboys-angels-first-chapter
for a sneak peek of what's next in the Cowboys
and Angels series.

Made in the USA
Columbia, SC
18 April 2018